JAGGER

THE HASTINGS SERIES #3

VANESSA SIENA

JAGGER

Copyright © 2020 by Vanessa Siena.
All rights reserved.
First Print Edition: June 2020

Limitless Publishing, LLC
Kailua, HI 96734
www.limitlesspublishing.com

Formatting: Book Pages By Design
Cover Design: Deranged Doctor Design

ISBN-13: 978-1-64034-890-5

DEDICATION

To Dad. I miss you.

PROLOGUE

Jagger

I felt her hands move over my chest, then, slowly, they made their way down to my stomach. Her fingers hooked into the hem of my shorts, which I put back on early this morning when the sun was barely shining through my bedroom window.

How she managed to slip into my bed is still a question I can't seem to answer. I thought I was done with her. We had our fun and all I wanted was to move on, not find her next to me completely naked.

I had my eyes still closed, knowing exactly what she wanted to do without looking at her. A blowjob was a nice thing to wake up to, that I wouldn't deny. But I promised myself last night that it was the last time I let her this close.

We fought too much, and when I tried to end it, she pulled the tears card on me. I hated it when women cried. Especially the ones who played the victim and acted like I was the bad guy in the situation.

But how was I supposed to turn her down in this situation? My cock was already hard, and I thought while she was still here, I could just let her do the job and then make her leave. Because that's how it worked between us. We had fun, then she'd leave.

"I know you're awake," she said in a challenging tone while she slowly pulled down my boxers. I took a deep breath, telling myself one more time that it would be the last time I'd see the sight of her head down there while her mouth worked my cock in a way only she knew how to.

I turned my head, opening my eyes, and looking directly into hers. "Make it quick," I told her and grabbed a handful of her hair, directing her mouth down to my dick. She smiled a little too excitedly, then lowered her head to lick along my length before she took the head into her mouth.

Starting slowly, she worked my cock with her right hand and moved her lips over my hardness. Then, with my hand pushing her down, she took it all in, making noises which in the beginning were a reason why I wanted to fuck her. She knew what she was doing, and she turned me on more than any other girl ever had. She was experienced. She had many men before she told me that she wanted to date me. But that was when it all started to fall apart. She thought she fell in love with me and I was stupid enough to let her believe I felt just the same. I didn't. I liked her. She was a friend and I knew she was someone I could trust. But now I was stuck in this situation and I wasn't man enough to tell her the truth and end it all.

"Fuck," I muttered through gritted teeth as I felt my cock hit the back of her throat. "Just like that." I lifted my other hand and grabbed another fistful of her hair. This time, I held her head tight and pushed it down. "Take it all." I knew it turned her on when I talked like that and it made her wild. She moved her head up and down faster, making my cock throb even more.

I felt the heat rise inside of me and I knew I was close. I also wanted her to leave. I was being an asshole, but I somehow needed to let her know that I had other things to do here, now that I moved to Newton, Kansas. It's a more than three-hour drive from Hastings, and I hoped to clear my head here, away from all the things that made me leave in the first place.

She was one of those reasons. Yet, I couldn't seem to stop myself from telling her where I went and giving her my new address.

The apartment I moved into was in an old, industrial building where they renovated the inside and built a few rentals. I liked how some of the walls had bricks showing and the high ceilings and big windows opened up the rooms and let in a lot of sunlight.

Unlike Hastings, Newton was a sunny town. The only problem with that was, ironically enough, on the day Dean died, it was the sunniest day in Hastings, so my thoughts went back to him each time the sun shone through my windows in the morning.

I tried not to think back to that day. Even if I had

shot many people in the past, killing Dean made me feel regret and self-hate for the first time.

Shaking off those thoughts, I looked back down to the girl who I wanted to forget just as much as October third. She looked up at me with my cock still deep inside her mouth and I knew she was trying to make me come any second. Lucky her, I only had to relax and shoot my shot. Literally.

"You gonna swallow like a good girl?" I asked, and she immediately nodded, then, enthusiastically moved even faster.

"Fuck," I groaned and kept her head in place to not miss her mouth. I didn't want my covers to get dirty, so she had to do what she was best at. It sounded all wrong and made me look like a dick, but she liked it. So why wouldn't I let her enjoy it?

"Are you at least going to let me get some coffee before I leave?" Her eyebrows were raised, and I gave her an annoyed look as I pulled up my boxers.

"I gotta get to work," I lied, because even after living in this town for over two months, I didn't feel the need to work or earn money. I had my money. Well, half of it. The other half I left Harlow. She was hesitant at first, but she finally gave in and told me she wouldn't use it for anything unless she really needed something.

She also didn't actually need the money since Hunter basically bought whatever they needed. They didn't leave Hastings. They re-opened Frankie's Diner and still lived in our old home. I asked Hunter why he wouldn't move into another house. One that's more fitted for them and a baby, but he told me that Harlow insisted on staying in

4

that house until she gave birth. She didn't want to go through any stressful moving situations and said that it would be bad for the baby. She was almost two months into the pregnancy, but she wasn't feeling very well. Morning sickness just didn't stop, and she also wouldn't stop working at the diner. My sister has always been a hard worker, but I don't think working that hard was good for the baby, either.

"And you don't even have time for one cup of coffee?" she asked me and put on the little red dress she wore yesterday. I shook my head, then grabbed clean clothes from my closet.

"No, Bliss. I don't have time for that, either." This was hard. She always tried to stay. She wouldn't leave until I stepped out of my front door myself, so this was like a routine for me. Waking up to her giving me a blowjob, telling her I needed to attend a job I didn't have, and make her leave and go back to Hastings. Not sure why she took on all those hours of driving just to be sent back home in the morning.

She sighed and put her hair into a messy bun, then grabbed her shoes and walked out of the bedroom. "You're an asshole," she mumbled, and I chuckled.

"No shit." I realized that back in Hastings. She was the only girl I fucked around with and it was okay the way it was. Just her and I, messing around in the sheets.

I followed her into the living room and watched her putting on her shoes. "When will you visit Harlow? It's been a while," she said.

I leaned against the wall next to the front door and shrugged. "Hunter's birthday is coming up. Harlow said something about a party. Might come by then."

Bliss gave me an amused look. "Hunter's birthday is in June."

I shrugged. "Yeah."

"That's in four months," she told me. I rolled my eyes and opened the door for her to get out. "Then I'll be back in four months."

Bliss watched me for some seconds, then walked up to me and put her hand on my chest. She smiled, leaned over, and kissed my lips. I didn't return the kiss, but I let her enjoy this little goodbye. She'd gotten used to it a little too much for my liking.

"I'll text you," she whispered. I just smiled, wishing I had the guts to tell her that I didn't want her to come back here.

CHAPTER ONE

Two weeks later

Jagger

I somehow managed to keep Bliss away from my apartment for the last week by telling her that I had shit to do and didn't have time for her to come around. She didn't take it personally. Lucky me. But she did tell me to text her as soon as I got time for her again.

I told her I wasn't sure it would be soon, and I guess that's a start, right? She'd eventually get bored and find herself another guy to have sex with. Why she was so stuck on me, I didn't quite understand. I treated her like shit, yet she still came around and acted like I was a saint.

I liked Bliss, but we had our differences, and when they showed it was always me who was at fault. Bliss only saw the bad in what I did when we fought, and to everyone else, it could look like she was the good girl in whatever relationship we were

7

having at the moment.

We fought too much considering we weren't even in a relationship or dating. I kept up with her bullshit too many times. When I was still in Hastings, and everything started between Bliss and me, I actually enjoyed her company. She was great to talk to and she knew how I felt thanks to Hunter, who did the same shit for a living as I did.

Killing people wasn't easy, and Bliss calmed me down in a way I didn't think was possible. She listened to my thoughts and tried to find a way for me to push them aside. It worked until she started acting like a crazy girlfriend, always asking where I was and who I was with. She was jealous of other girls I talked to at bars and I didn't understand why since she didn't hold back on flirting with other guys, either.

I should've told her what we had was over, but then, the sex was great, and she was naïve enough not to realize that for me it was just pure pleasure. The girl had to fall on her face one day and make those pink glasses fall to the ground to see clearly and realize that I didn't share the same feelings as she did. Sure, I could just simply tell her, but she would freak out. I was in too deep already and I knew Bliss and her temper. You wouldn't want to be around when she got mad.

"Need some help there, buddy?" An amused voice broke through my thoughts and I turned to see a girl standing by the staircase with two large bags, one in each hand.

"What?" I asked and got a smirk from her.

"Do you need some help? You've been standing

in front of your door for several minutes and still haven't opened it. This is my second time walking up here and you're still in the same spot."

Shit. See? Bliss was taking up too much space in my head. I needed her out of there as soon as possible.

I looked down at the keys in my hand and then shook my head, letting out a small chuckle. "Deep thoughts," I told her and turned back to look at her. "You need some help with that?" I then asked and nodded toward her groceries.

She shrugged and smiled. "I got some beer outside next to my car."

I pushed the keys back into my pocket and walked toward the stairs. "What apartment?" I asked. "One floor up," she told me and started walking up the stairs.

I nodded again, making my way down and out to her car, which I recognized by the two full crates of beer. I picked them both up, one with each hand, and walked back inside the apartment complex and up the stairs to the second floor, where her door was wide open.

"You having a party?" I asked and walked right into her home since she pretty much invited me by leaving the door open.

"Yes," she answered and walked toward me with a wide smile on her face. "Tonight. You can come. It's gonna be fun." She grinned and grabbed one of the crates, then walked back into the kitchen and I followed her.

"Unless you're too busy thinking about whatever you were thinking down there." She was making fun of me and well, I didn't blame her.

"I think I'll come by and grab a beer," I told her and looked around. Her apartment was the same as mine, yet she had way more furniture and decor around the place. I should ask Harlow if she'd like to help out with my place. It was almost empty, and it looked sad with all the spaces I could fill.

"I'm Sage, by the way." I looked back at her and shook her hand. "Jagger. Nice place. I like the paintings," I told her and took another look around.

"Yeah? My cousin made them for me. She's super talented. She also takes requests," Sage explained with a proud smile. "She'll be here tonight. In case you want to ask her about more of her work. I got a glance into your apartment once and it looks a little...boring."

I laughed and looked back at her. "It is boring. I'll make sure to ask your cousin about her paintings."

"Perfect. Now, get out. I gotta get ready for tonight. People will be here around nine."

Attending a party was exactly what I needed. In the end, that's what I came here for, right? To meet new people and keep the bad thoughts out of my mind. Sage seemed like a nice girl and going to that party would help me make some new friends.

It was almost nine. I pulled a black t-shirt over my head as my phone vibrated on the kitchen counter. *Please don't let that be Bliss,* I prayed. When I reached my phone, I saw Harlow's name on the screen and relaxed a little before picking up.

"Hey, sweet girl. How's the baby?" I asked and leaned against the counter. Harlow's calls always made me happy.

"It's growing too fast," she told me with a smile I could hear in her voice. "Hunter jokes about my belly being too big for two months and he says he's not sure if I'm actually pregnant or just eating too much." She chuckled.

I laughed, shaking my head. "Tell that idiot he should watch his mouth, or I'll come over there and make sure he won't be able to walk straight for the rest of your pregnancy." I was obviously joking, and I knew Harlow didn't take it seriously, either.

Her laugh lit up my whole mood. Thank God she was doing okay. And Hunter was being good to her. "I wouldn't mind you coming here for a day or two, you know?"

I sighed, knowing a visit was long overdue. "I promise I'll come by soon. I just need some more time here, all right?"

She was silent for a while, then she finally spoke. "We miss you, Jag. But I understand your hesitation. Take your time, okay?"

"I miss you too. I'll let you know as soon as I'm ready. And if you can't wait to see me any longer, let me know and I'll have my guest bedroom ready for you and Hunter. I know it's a long drive and you don't want to leave the diner, but I'd love for you to see my apartment. You'll love it."

"I'll talk to Hunter about it. I gotta go. We've got a sixteenth birthday party here at the diner and it's time for cake," she told me, and I smiled, knowing how much kids liked the diner. Harlow and Hunter had a lot to do every day since people filled that place from the early morning on.

"Have fun. And tell Hunter not to let you work so damn hard. That baby and its momma need a rest too," I said into the phone.

"I will. I love you," she replied and then hung up. I was happy for them. But all those hearts and flowers made me feel sick to my stomach. The only love I felt was for my sister and admittedly, I loved Hunter too. He's officially part of the family now. Not just my best friend.

I heard music coming from speakers upstairs and I knew it was time to meet some new people. I was ready and I intended to make friends tonight.

Sage was a good start. She was kind enough to invite a stranger to her party, so that must've meant people in Newton were more open-minded and welcoming. Not judging by appearance or wealth. So, I was ready. Ready to meet new faces.

CHAPTER TWO

Jagger

The door to Sage's apartment was open and I heard voices and music coming from the inside. Since she did invite me earlier, I decided to just enter and look around. Before reaching her living room, two girls came out of the bathroom and almost bumped into me. They laughed, then gave me flirtatious smiles and made their way back to the almost overcrowded living room. If those girls wouldn't have smelled like a full bottle of vodka, I might've smiled back. I wasn't into those kinds of girls. Sure, they were easy. And I did sometimes like the easy kind, yet a challenge was far more fun and intriguing. But at the moment, I didn't have the time or need for women anyway.

I made my way over to the small bar that was probably built by someone Sage knew. It wasn't perfectly built, and it didn't look very stable, either, but it held bottles and cans and also some buckets with ice, so it did the trick.

I grabbed myself a beer and opened the bottle by holding the cap of it against an edge of the piece of wood from the bar, then slammed my hand over it so the cap fell off easily. It was a dick move since there was a bottle opener right next to me, but hell, I was allowed to have some fun.

"Impressive." Sage's familiar voice chimed from behind me and I turned to look at her. "Is that your party trick?" she mocked. I laughed and shrugged before taking a sip of my beer.

"Gets lots of girls' panties wet," I explained sarcastically. Luckily, Sage had a good sense of humor and didn't take my stupid response seriously.

"I see. So, you came. There's some finger food over there and I ordered pizza for later. Make yourself at home." I looked around the living room and noticed now how much she actually put into this party. She decorated some walls and furniture and the music was coming from an old jukebox. Impressive.

"Thanks. I will," I told her and looked back at her. She was about to say something when she turned to look at a guy walking into her living room with a bottle of Jack in his hand and a huge cocky smile on his face. He reached Sage and picked her up by wrapping his free arm around her back.

"You came!" Sage laughed, and the guy put her back down on her feet. "Here, let me introduce you to my new neighbor. Well, he's been around some weeks now, but I never got to meet him. Joey, this is Jagger. He lives downstairs. Jagger, this is Joey. My boyfriend." Joey and I shook hands and I nodded toward Sage. "How do you keep up with a

14

crazy one like her?" Deep inside, I was hoping he wouldn't take it seriously.

Joey eyed me for a second before he let out a hard laugh, wrapping his arm around Sage's shoulders now. "If I ever find out, I'll let you know." He grinned and then turned to his girlfriend, who couldn't stop beaming at him. See, that's what I would never want. Someone who adored the shit out of you. That wasn't going to happen to me because I didn't want it to. Well, I did have Harlow, whom I adored just as much as she adored me. But that's different. We have a history. And she's the only one who'll ever understand and accept me for my past.

"Sadie is looking for you. She's in the kitchen." Sage nodded and stood on her tiptoes to kiss Joey on the lips. "I'll be right back. And don't start drinking without me," she warned him and then disappeared in the crowd.

I took another sip of my beer and turned to watch some girls dance. They were all dressed in either shorts and a t-shirt, or a nice little summer dress. Yeah, those girls were going to be easy. And maybe one of them would help me get Bliss off my mind completely. But not tonight. I didn't want to be known as the new guy in town who fucks around.

"Distracting, right?" Joey said beside me and when I looked at him, his eyes were on the same three girls I was just watching. "They're trying to get our attention and before you know it, they got you naked and above them." I was confused as to why he was talking about having sex with those girls when he clearly was in a relationship with

Sage.

I nodded slowly, puckering my lips to hide my confusion. "I know those types." I didn't need to say more. Instead, I kept drinking my beer and enjoying the music. Joey didn't seem like the type of guy I needed to become close with, but Sage was nice, so I couldn't just leave him standing there alone when he clearly tried to start a conversation with me.

"Ah, there he is," Joey then said and pointed toward a tall, blond guy. He walked toward us and greeted Joey with a fist bump before turning to me and holding his hand out for me to take. I shook it and immediately noticed his crooked nose. Must've been broken one too many times.

"I'm Dallas," he introduced himself and I nodded once. "Jagger." Dallas seemed a little calmer and relaxed. Laid back. He was more my speed. "You new around here?" he then asked and leaned against the bar next to me, grabbing a beer too.

"I moved in a few weeks ago. I live downstairs," I explained and was surprisingly relieved when Joey left us to go look for Sage.

"Nice place, huh? I live one floor up. I wasn't in town though for the last three months." I turned to look at him and studied his face. Something about him looked familiar. My eyes dropped down to his hands and that's when I saw the bruises on his knuckles and two fingers that were a hundred percent broken recently.

"Dallas Washington," I said, getting his full attention now. He nodded, an amused grin

16

spreading on his lips now. "The one and only."

I chuckled and shook my head. "Pleasure to meet you, man," I told him. "You've seen some of my fights?" he asked and took a long sip from his beer.

"One, yeah. In Hastings. But that was years ago. Shit, man, I was close to getting in that fucking ring to beat you up," I joked.

Dallas Washington's an underground fighter. He was known for his fights and people tried to win against him. None of them ever did, though. They lost all their bidding money because they were sure that one day, someone would kick his ass.

One night, when I was still fighting myself, I heard about Dallas coming to Hastings and I wanted to go against him. That was before I met Hunter and back then I wasn't as good as I became later.

Dallas let out a laugh and turned to look at me with amusement in his eyes. "You still fight?" he asked, challenging me. I shook my head. "Stopped some years ago. Had some family issues going on."

"Too bad. But then, I would probably just put you to the ground faster than you'd think."

That made me laugh. Because he was probably right. "I'll come and watch one of your fights, though."

"Good, you're back," Sage stated and looked up at Dallas. "Gray will freak out when she sees you. Not in a good way. You should've called her," she added.

"She'll understand," Dallas said, suddenly annoyed with her. "Is she here?"

Sage nodded, pointing in a direction where a girl with fiery red hair was walking toward us, her eyes set on Dallas and a deep frown between her brows.

"Your girlfriend?" I asked. Dallas chuckled and shook his head. "Nah, my little sister."

I could work with that. Maybe, after all, I could get to know one girl who would show me a good time. Gray, as they called her, suddenly sparked some interest in me. Her hair distracted me. Her expressive blue eyes were another thing telling me to get to know her better.

"I was worried sick!" Gray's voice was full of disappointment mixed with relief and a tiny bit of anger. Not just her hair was fiery, but her attitude was dynamic, and I wanted more of that.

With a push against Dallas's chest, she stomped her foot for emphasis and propped her hands on her hips, showing him just how mad she was. Damn, I liked that girl already.

"I missed you too, Rusty," Dallas said with delight in his voice. I wasn't sure if it was okay to laugh at the silly nickname, but then, Sage and Joey couldn't hold back a chuckle, either.

Gray's eyes shot up at me and she looked a little unsure how to react to a stranger laughing at her nickname, which was, fair enough, very fitting.

She tore her eyes off me again to look at Dallas, then her face fell and relaxed and her arms crossed over her chest. "Next time, make sure to tell me when you leave town."

"I will. Now, turn that frown upside down and grab a beer, sis. Party's just starting."

Their relationship seemed to be fun and tight. I had a tight relation with Harlow too. But if I ever called Low by a stupid nickname like that, she would probably get offended. I liked how easygoing Gray was.

I decided I wanted to talk to her too. I took a step forward and held out my hand for her to take. "I'm Jagger. It's nice to meet you."

Her eyes went straight to my hand and I could tell she was trying to decide if I was safe or just some random guy who wanted to get inside her panties...because that's what I imagined guys wanted to do with her. Gray was a different kind of beautiful. Rare and pure. Her freckles around her nose seemed almost aggressive with the contrast of her pale skin, but with her long hair and those naturally red lips, it all tied together perfectly.

She still didn't take my hand, but her eyes were on mine now. She studied my face and probably saw the amusement in my eyes. I could tell the others were watching us and my attempt to introduce myself to her. I was making a fool out of myself. Great.

But Gray then decided to go ahead and make the situation even worse for me, but funnier for the others. She smiled at me with a fake, devilish smile, then tilted her head to the side and said: "Rusty."

With that, she turned on her heel, reaching for Sage's arm and pulling her into the crowd.

Damn, that girl knew how to leave a good first impression.

CHAPTER THREE

Gray

I felt his eyes on me the whole time. I was dancing with Sage, and to be fair, neither of us were great dancers. So he might've been staring at us to entertain himself. My dance moves were horrible and not sexy at all, which was my way to keep guys far away from me.

Most guys in this town knew me personally and they all saw me as their friend. Their funny, kind friend who was always up for a party but never down to fuck. That's what Joey once said to me in front of Sage and Dallas. But then, Joey was an asshole and I still didn't understand why Sage wouldn't dump him. Sure, he was good looking, but his way of expressing himself was terrible.

To me, every man was pretty much useless unless they could show me what good there was in dating them. I didn't want a relationship just to rub it in others' faces and say: "Hey, look, I have sex every now and then and you don't." I never felt the need to sleep with one of them just because they were hot. Now, I did enjoy some men's company. They were fun, and most of them were great to talk to, but they never seemed to spark interest in me the way Joey did in Sage. I wanted to stay on the safe side and be the girl who's free, strong, and independent.

"He can't take his eyes off you," Sage whispered in my ear as she leaned in, still moving her body to the music. I turned to look in the direction Sage and Dallas's new neighbor was standing, looking directly into Jagger's eyes.

See, that's my dilemma. Men wanted me. They always saw me as a challenge, considering I wasn't like the other girls. Sure, that last sentence was *so cliché*, but I knew for a fact most girls would've acknowledged Jagger's flirting and probably ended up in his bed after the party was over. I had a different approach to guys like him. I let them stare, dream about what they would do to me, and then I'd explain to them why I wouldn't let them in my panties.

"Let's grab a drink," I replied to Sage and pulled her into the kitchen. Some people were taking shots and others were watching with beers in their hands. Sage's parties were always wild, and thanks to Joey's connection to Newton College, a whole bunch of people attended.

I opened the fridge, knowing Sage stored some more drinks in there, and I grabbed two bottles of Smirnoff Ice. I loved that stuff. I wasn't a heavy drinker, but I enjoyed getting slightly drunk now and then. I drank responsibly, not like Sage. She ended up passed out on the kitchen floor more than once at her parties. Luckily, Joey was kind enough to carry her to bed.

After opening the bottles, we made our way outside to the fairly big balcony which was connected to the kitchen. No one was out there, but people had been smoking before, hence the filled ashtrays on the small table. We sat down on the couch and Sage immediately grabbed her pack of cigarettes out of her back pocket and lit one. As her best friend and cousin, I should've been telling her to stop smoking. But with Sage, it was never a good idea to tell her so. Smoking was her way of getting back at her parents for kicking her out of the house when she was seventeen. She was a bit of a rebel and her parents were uptight. Her dad, my uncle Will, has always been strict.

I lucked out. My dad always supported me and my decisions, and even if I most times helped Sage out with her sneaking out late at night, he never got mad at me. Dad was more easygoing than his brother. It also showed in their marriages.

Uncle Will and Aunt Faye were high school sweethearts and got married right after college. You could tell that they've been married for a long time by the way they acted around one another. They didn't hold or kiss each other anymore and their attitudes were almost cold.

My parents were different. Dad had Dallas with a woman I never met. Dallas was still little when dad divorced his mother and some years later, after raising Dallas on his own, Dad met my mom. Dad married her and quickly after, I was born. Even if he wasn't my mother's son, my mom took Dallas in and even got him adopted. So, even if Dallas technically was my half-brother, I saw him as my real one. That would also explain my red hair and blue eyes, and Dallas's very blond hair and green eyes. We also didn't really look alike. We just got the same sense of humor from Dad, which helped me deal with Dallas's nicknames he gave me.

"Mind if I join you?" I didn't even get to talk to Sage alone and yet, there he was.

"No, not at all," Sage answered Jagger and he smiled, sitting down on the chair next to her. "Smoke?" Sage asked, holding out her cigarettes for him to take.

Jagger shook his head and gave a crooked grin. "Trying to stop," he explained. I chuckled and eyed him. He doesn't seem so bad. He was being nice, and I shouldn't have any prejudices toward him.

"Sage told me you paint," Jagger started the conversation. I took a glance at Sage, who shrugged, then I looked back at Jagger and nodded.

"Yes. Well, I'm not a pro but...turns out people actually like my work."

"No, it's amazing. I could use some artwork in my apartment. It's dull right now. Maybe you could show me some of your paintings someday," he told me with a smile.

I returned his smile and decided that he wasn't as bad as I thought. He was being nice, so I nodded in agreement. "Where are you from?" I then asked.

"Hastings," he replied, then quickly added "Nebraska."

"And what made you come over here?" Sage

asked, taking the last drag of her cigarette before putting it out in the ashtray.

"Family," was his simple answer. It didn't seem like he wanted to go deeper into that matter, so I wanted to change the subject. Dallas stepped outside and interrupted my plan.

"Still don't get why you're with that idiot in there." Dallas pointed the bottom of his bottle toward Joey, who was chugging a beer, and others were cheering him on. He then handed Jagger another beer and sat down next to him. Sage shrugged. "Mom and Dad hate him."

"Ah, right. You're still getting back at them." Dallas laughed and shook his head. "Can't wait for you to hear them fight almost daily. These walls are thinner than you think," Dallas explained and took a sip of his beer.

Jagger let out a chuckle, then he shrugged. "I think I've heard worse than fighting." His eyes then landed on mine, and with a smile, he asked, "Where do you live?"

"Five-minute walk from here. I had the chance to move into your apartment when it was still empty, but I wanted to get some distance between them and myself."

Dallas and Sage both let out hard laughs. "But you still spend most of your time here with us," Sage pointed out. I rolled my eyes but couldn't hide a grin. She was right. I did like spending time with them.

"Means I'll see you more often, then." Jagger wasn't holding back on flirting with me, even with my brother and my cousin next to us. His flirting was so subtle though, that I didn't mind. I liked it. He wasn't pushing me in any way, and he was testing my limits and how far he could go. He was respecting me. That was different and nice for a change.

CHAPTER FOUR

Jagger

I was having a good time and talking to my new neighbors was very entertaining. I learned that Gray and Dallas had the same father, but not the same mother, that's why Sage's only cousin to Gray. I also found out that the three of them pretty much spent their whole childhood together up to now. They never left each other's sides, which is nice.

Gray got quieter the later it got, and I could tell she was tired. I watched her from time to time to make sure she wouldn't fall asleep right there on the couch outside. I wondered if she stayed at Sage's overnight or not.

To assure me she wasn't falling asleep, Gray gave me a small smile here and then. I smiled back, looking at her face a little closer. She was pretty. But then, she knew. But even though she was aware of her beauty, she didn't flaunt it. That made her as a person even more interesting. She was down to earth, yet she wasn't afraid to speak her mind.

"You staying here?" I asked her when Dallas and Sage went inside to grab another drink and make sure Joey wouldn't down another bottle of vodka. *What an idiot*, I thought. Surely, Sage wasn't in love with him the way Harlow was in love with Hunter. It was a different kind of love.

"No," Gray answered and sat up straight, reaching for her drink and taking the last sip. "I have to do some work tomorrow, so I need to get some sleep."

I nodded, then slightly pushed my phone out of the pocket to check the time. "It's getting late for me too. Would you like me to walk you home?" At first, the question sounded stupid and creepy, but Gray's smile changed the way it sounded.

"That would be nice," she told me and pressed her lips together to hide a grin. I nodded, relieved that I didn't make a fool out of myself.

"Let's go then," I suggested, and Gray quickly got up, stretching for a second and putting on her jacket. Just as we were about to walk back inside, Dallas came our way and looked at us with a questioning look. "Already leaving?" he asked and Gray and I nodded simultaneously. Dallas then looked at me. "Taking her home?"

"Yeah," was my only response. I wanted to ask if he wanted to take her himself since he's her brother, but I didn't want to miss the chance to get to know her a little better.

Dallas was silent for a second, then he nodded. "See you around," he told Gray and passed us to go back outside to the balcony.

As we stepped back inside, there were still a lot

of people in Sage's apartment. If I wasn't mistaken, even more people arrived after ten. I must've stopped walking when I realized there wasn't a way to get out of there without pushing past everyone because Gray's hand grabbed mine, pulling me through the crowd. I guess that was one way of doing it. But in my experience, when a guy like me pushed through a crowd like that, other guys thought I wanted to start a fight.

Gray's hand never left mine as we made our way to the door, and even after leaving the apartment, she kept on holding on. "Sage's parties are pretty wild," she explained with an apologetic grin and I shrugged.

"It was fun," I told her, getting a better look at her now that we were under some bright lights in the stairwell. She smiled now and looked down at our conjoined hands. She wasn't going to let go if a too damn familiar voice hadn't broken through our silence.

"Good reason to ignore my texts," Bliss said in a voice I wanted to be able to just get out of my system. Her eyes were focused on me, but I knew she was directing her almost arrogant, angry tone at Gray. Her hand quickly left mine and then she buried both her hands into her jacket.

I rolled my eyes because I couldn't hide my annoyance. "What are you doing here?" I asked, shoving my fists into my front pockets to hide my tension.

"I came to see you. What else would I be doing here at almost one in the morning?" she shot back.

I wasn't having it. Not right now. I pulled out the

key to my apartment and held it out for her to take. "Go wait inside. I'm walking Gray home." I wanted to let Bliss know that I wasn't keeping up with her bullshit and that I wasn't stuck to her. I had my own life. A new one. One I wanted to have to get away from my old one. But that wasn't going to work with her showing up here unannounced every now and then.

Bliss's eyebrow raised and she gave me a look that said: *"are you fucking kidding me?"*.

Quite frankly, I wasn't. "Go, Bliss. Gray needs to get home and I'm going with her." I tried not to sound too annoyed. I didn't want to scare Gray off or make her think I was a total asshole.

Bliss let out a snort, which sounded stupid, to begin with, then she turned on her heels and walked back down the stairs. I heard her open my apartment, then shut the door a tad bit too forcefully and locking herself in.

I sighed, running a hand through my hair, and looking over at Gray. She seemed amused. "Your girlfriend?" she asked, seemingly untouched by Bliss's behavior.

I shook my head and let out a laugh. "Just an old friend," I explained, but Gray didn't really seem to buy that answer.

"An old friend you fucked frequently," she added, surprising me with her words. She didn't seem like the girl to use vulgar language, but something about it was amusing.

The corners of my mouth lifted slowly and then I nodded. "Some months ago. She's my best friend's sister. It's complicated," I told her and started

29

walking down the stairs. Gray followed me and puckered her lips to indicate she was thinking about something. After we exited the building, she looked up at the windows and pressed her lips into a thin line before letting out a chuckle.

I didn't look up because I knew what she was seeing. And she was enjoying it. "She's looking out the window, isn't she?" I asked, not able to hold back a chuckle myself.

"Maybe," Gray answered, and to provoke Bliss just a little more, she grabbed my hand and lifted my arm to wrap around her shoulders. This time I laughed, shaking my head but pulling her closer to my side. "You're pushing me deeper in that puddle of shit this way, you know that?" I asked but couldn't help from kissing the top of her head.

I expected my move to feel wrong since Gray and I met just hours ago. But somehow, it felt right having her this close. I wasn't just using her to make Bliss jealous. Well, to be fair, Gray started it. But I knew I wanted to hold her like this again after tonight.

"She seems nice. But I can tell you're not feeling what she's feeling."

That sentence made me look down at her with interest and a little bit of confusion. "You think she's got feelings for me?" I asked.

Gray rolled her eyes and nodded. "God, why do men not notice that? I mean, she's jealous of me and probably thinks we're having sex. She's hurt because you ignored her texts and she came all the way here, at night, to see you. My advice? Tell her what you really feel. Because I don't think she knows and that's not fair."

Of course, she was right. But it wasn't as easy as it sounded. Sure, being honest was important. But Bliss was different. If I'd tell her off, she would make sure my life would be hell from that moment on and I wasn't up for that bullshit.

I kept quiet because I didn't know what to say to that. I knew I should be doing exactly that right after getting back home, but I was sure I wouldn't.

Gray noticed my silence and knew she shouldn't keep on talking about that matter anymore. "And, hey," she then said, lightly punching my stomach. "You can't just ignore someone's texts. That's rude. If you'd ignore my texts, I'd probably block you immediately." She grinned and stopped walking. She pointed to a door. "That's me."

I stepped away from her to give her some space, then pushed my hands back into my pockets. I smiled at her, tilting my head to the side. "For that, I would need your phone number," I said.

She let out a laugh and reached into the pocket of her jacket and pulled out a bundle of keys. "Very smooth." She smiled and then nodded in my direction, indicating me to go back home. "I'll let you have my number as soon as you've talked to Bliss. She deserves that. And I don't want someone who's got business going on with another girl."

I could tell she was being serious. And she was also right.

"I will," I told her with all honesty.

"Good. I'll see you around." And with that, she opened the door and went inside with one last glance back at me.

One thing was for sure: I liked her and because of her, I was going to confront Bliss tonight.

CHAPTER FIVE

Jagger

I found Bliss sitting on my couch with a beer bottle in her hand and an annoyed but tired expression on her face. I wondered why she came here out of the blue. For sex? Because she missed me? I didn't see a point in any of those two reasons. Mostly because she hadn't heard from me in a while and I didn't ask her to come.

I sighed at her eyeing me as I took off my jacket and hung it on the hook at the back of my front door. "Where did you get that beer?" I asked, knowing I didn't have that type of beer in my fridge. She raised a brow, then leaned back and took long sips of her bottle. "I met some of your new friends upstairs. They seem nice," she told me in a challenging voice. What the fuck was that for? It's not like I was fucking any of them. Even if that was the case, she had no right to act this way.

"They are. Really nice, actually," I shot back and stood there in front of the couch, my arms crossed and my eyes on hers. "Why are you here, Bliss?" I finally asked, thinking at the back of my mind that I was doing this for a girl I just met. A girl who stunned me by just being herself and not trying to flirt or get noticed by anyone.

"Because last time I came here you told me your door was open and I could come whenever I wanted."

Well, that was a big fat lie from her side. "I never said those words. Last time you were here I told you I didn't have time for you. Or us. Whatever this between us was."

It somehow felt good telling her all that but her hurt expression made it all worse. Fucking great.

"Was?" she asked silently, knowing exactly how sad she could sound with her manipulative voice. One thing most people didn't know about Bliss was, that she was a master at playing with people's minds. She was good at twisting things people said in a way that would only benefit her and make others feel weak and wrong. That shit didn't work with me. I've been there before. Not happening again.

"Yes. Past tense," I explained in a mocking tone. "We were fucking. What the hell did you think was going to happen between us? We've known each other for years and we basically started fucking because I was mad at Hunter for sleeping with my sister."

That one punched her right in the face. Upfront and with full force. But I had to get that shit straight. I was done playing her games.

"And you never had the guts to open up like that

34

about your feelings before I fell in love with you?"
This time I laughed. Fucking hell. Did she really
wanna go down that road and pull the love-card on
me?

"Bullshit," I breathed and shook my head,
running my hand through my hair and pulling at the
ends to release some stress that was building up
inside of me.

"You don't love me," I pointed out and watched
her get up from the couch, leaving her beer on the
small table between us. She walked around it,
keeping her eyes on mine and Jesus Christ, was she
actually going to cry now too?

I let out a harsh laugh and took a few steps back
to gain some distance between us again. "How
would you know? You never asked how I was
feeling. What I felt for you, to be clearer." She
stopped a few feet away, mimicking my stance and
crossing her arms over her chest. Her eyes were
watering, and, in some seconds, there would be
tears running down her cheeks. What a talented
little actress she was.

"You knew we were just fucking, Bliss. We were
having fun and that's it. You knew that from the
start and in the beginning it worked. So why
weren't you the one to stop it? To step back and tell
me we couldn't do this anymore because you were
catching feelings?" I had my fair points and I saw a
little flash in her eyes telling me what I was saying
was the truth.

I waited for her to answer but she just stood there
in silence. I sighed, knowing that in moments like
this I would have to be the one to say something

35

first. She was stubborn, and if I wanted her out of my apartment, I had to make the first step. Once again.

"I'm sorry," I started and thought about what I wanted to say next. "But this has been going on for too long and I should've stopped a long time ago. I moved here to get away from everything happening in Hastings. After Dean's death, all I wanted to do was move far away and stay on the down-low to start over again and be alone with my thoughts. I couldn't move too far because I didn't want Low to worry." That was a good apology, right? I was being honest. A little too late, but better late than never.

"So...I was a distraction," she said in a monotone, her tone not matching the teary eyes.

I chuckled because I couldn't believe she was pulling that shit on me. "Yes. And you knew you were. We talked about that the first night I was at your place. After Harlow's accident. I came to you to talk and you offered me to stay at your place to distract myself. Hell, you literally offered to sleep with me to make me feel better."

Everything I was saying was honesty at its finest, and Bliss knew. She lowered her head, staring at her hands while playing with her fingers. This time I sighed and reached out to touch her shoulder. When I realized it was a shitty gesture, I moved my hand up and with two fingers, I lifted her chin, so she had to look at me. "You can't play with me like that, Bliss. I know you too well. I'm done playing. And again, I'm sorry if I hurt you in any way. It wasn't my intention. I just had to grow a pair to tell you."

She studied my face after I stopped talking and swallowed hard before nodding. "It's okay, I guess," she told me and shrugged it off quickly. "I mean, I was naïve. I just liked being close to you."

I nodded, pressing my lips into a thin line, and cursing myself for not being able to keep her at a distance when she was acting this way. I pulled her to me and hugged her to my chest.

"We can be friends, right?" she asked quietly. Thank fuck for that. I didn't want her to go back home and stay angry at me for the rest of her life.

"Of course. I just…need some space, you know? I haven't been able to find myself yet." Shooting Dean turned some sort of switch inside of me and now all I felt inside was emptiness. It's not that I wasn't feeling anything at all, I just didn't know who I really was anymore. The shooting itself wasn't the problem. I killed people in the past. Was a coldhearted killer. But killing your own father was hard, even if he dragged you and your little sister through hell half your lives.

Bliss didn't answer me, and I thought it was best if we just stopped talking about that matter. I let her go from my embrace and looked down at her with a small smile. "It's late." With that, I intended to go to sleep as soon as possible.

"Do you want me to sleep on the couch?" she asked, a challenging tone escaping her again. No, I didn't want her to sleep on the couch. But I didn't want to sleep in my bed with her, either. If I was going to put boundaries between us, then I had to start with it right now.

"No, I'll take the couch." I nodded toward the

bedroom. "Go on. You know where all the things are." Bliss slowly nodded and to my surprise, her eyes were back to normal. Almost emotionless and not sad at all.

I think she just had to get it right in her head and tell herself that she didn't love me the way she thought she did. I saw it on her face. She just needed someone to make her feel appreciated. I could give her that, but without sex. Or feelings.

"Okay, goodnight then," she said and gave me a quick smile before walking toward my bedroom door. A sigh of relief escaped me, and I let my head fall back, closing my eyes and thanking Gray for pushing me to talk to Bliss.

Sure, I was happy to have made up with Bliss and talk it out, but I was more excited about Gray's number, which she promised to give me when I was done with this all.

So tomorrow, I'd make sure to visit Gray at work.

CHAPTER SIX

Jagger

"Sorry I don't have any more to eat here. I usually go out and grab something at the bakery or coffee shop," I told Bliss as she took another bite of her apple.

She shrugged, leaned against the kitchen counter, crossing one arm over her chest. "I'll find a drive-through on my way back to Hastings. What are you up to today?" she then asked and tilted her head.

My plan for today was to visit Gray at work. She told me yesterday where her little studio is, and I wasn't hesitating on seeing her again. After last night, she left a very sweet and positive impression and I couldn't seem to shake her off my mind.

"I gotta run some errands." My answer was simple, and I didn't feel like she had to know exactly what my schedule for the day looked like. "Do you need some money for gas? It's a long drive back home." The least I could do was to offer her something more than just a damn apple. In the end, she still worked at that diner on the highway. Even though Hunter paid her rent, I was sure she was barely getting by with the money she made. And gas was expensive.

"I got it," she told me and took the last bite before throwing what was left of the apple into the bin. Of course, she wouldn't accept any of my money either. I had too much of it and I had no idea what to do with it. Low and Hunter used it to renovate Frankie's Diner and they also sent some to Frankie's family after the funeral. They had a job and a new life. But I wasn't sure what I was going to do with my life yet. Working for Gunner had been fun but exhausting. Leaving his business was the first step into the normal world. Well, I did have a job at the mechanic's in Hastings, but I mostly did it to get my mind off shit that was bothering me. It was more of a hobby than a job. Now, I was in Newton-fucking-Kansas and I had no clue about what my life would end up being like.

"You got everything?" I followed Bliss to the front door and reached into my jacket, pulling out my wallet and taking out a hundred-dollar bill. Without saying a word, I pushed the bill into her back pocket and gave her a warning look, not to start complaining. She sighed and shook her head. "Just remember that every cent you give me will come back to you someday." At least she wasn't like some girls, greedy for money and all shiny things.

"Until that day comes, you'll forget about it," I grinned and nodded toward the door. "Drive safe," I added, and to be fully honest, I wasn't sure what to do. Luckily, Bliss did the first move and grabbed her bag, put her hand on my shoulder, and then left with a quick goodbye. She didn't complicate things after last night and I was somewhat positive that she accepted what I told her. That was a big step, even for Bliss. Normally, she would start bitchin' around but this time, she just let it slip.

***

The street to Gray's little art studio was located near a railway and the building she said wasn't a big deal was impressively large. The small sign next to the entrance door said: "Gray Washington's Art Gallery & Studio" and the open sign had a creative twist to it with its background painted as Van Gogh's *Starry Night*. I couldn't help but smile and I was sure I looked like a fool, grinning at a damn sign.

Since it was an open building for people to go in and view her paintings, and maybe buy them, I pulled the door toward me and entered the slightly cool room. The AC was on and I remembered Gray saying that she usually wears a sweater to work, since the heat could destroy her painting. It was a little chilly, but I didn't mind. I looked around and the big paintings on the walls immediately caught my interest. I'd seen her work before at Sage's house, but these were different. More realistic and rather detailed compared to the abstract ones I'd already seen.

"I really hope you talked to Bliss and clarified things with her before coming here." Her voice made me grin wider and I turned to see her standing a few feet away from me with a large brush in her left hand.

"Of course I did. And now I'm ready to get to know you better." I glanced around again and pushed my hands into my pockets. "You're incredibly talented, Miss Washington. Great name, by the way," I pointed out.

Gray chuckled and then nodded. "Sadly, George Washington is not a relative of mine. Guess I just lucked out with the name."

I let out a small laugh and took some steps closer, closing the space between us. "It's really nice to see you in daylight. You think I could now actually count all those freckles on your face?" I had no idea what had gotten into me. Where did that cheesy talk come from? I was good at flirting with girls but never had I said something corny like that. Shit.

I expected Gray to laugh or push me off, but she smiled sweetly and shrugged to answer my stupid question. "You can try. The last few guys got to around forty." That's when it hit me. She was being sarcastic and that only made me want to get closer. Fuck, she was lighting up something in me that I couldn't explain.

I chuckled this time and shook my head, reaching out my hands to grab her by the waist and pull her close. I wasn't going to kiss her, because then I would've probably gotten a smack across the face, but I did want to hold her. Like last night, when she put my arm around her shoulder and snuggled up against my side. That was nice. I wanted that again.

"Are you fucking with me?" I asked teasingly and lifted an eyebrow. She shrugged once more and smirked. "Maybe. But I actually did try to count them once when I was little."

"And how many did you count?" She wasn't backing up, which meant she enjoyed being close too. Good. I needed that right now.

"Don't remember. I fell asleep and never tried again." And before I knew it, something wet and cold touched my cheek. "You got something there," she said, scrunching up her nose and pointing to my cheek with her brush. She then wiggled out of my arms and walked toward an open door, probably where she came from before.

I grinned and shook my head, knowing there was a big blue stain on my cheek. This girl was something else. Her bubbly, fun temper was intriguing, and I wanted to be around her more. I followed her and couldn't help but glance at her butt. Sure, that was a shit move, but she did have a nice body. She wasn't skinny, yet her curves were just enough to make me want to run my hands over them all day long. Her hair was in a loose ponytail and I loved the way it moved when she walked.

"Are you busy right now? I would like to take you out to lunch."

"As in a date?" she asked and stopped in front of a painting sitting on an easel.

I eyed the still mostly unpainted canvas and nodded. "Yes. I mean, Bliss is out of the picture. I explained how I feel about the thing we had, and she took it well. So, yes, I wanna take you out on a lunch date."

Gray puckered her lips and studied the canvas in front of her, then turned to look at me with a smile. "I think I'll pass."

Her answer surprised me and at first, I thought she was being sarcastic again. "Why?" It almost sounded like a whine and I could've punched myself for that. *Jesus, man up, Jagger.*

"Because no good restaurant is open at lunchtime and I would rather let you take me to a nice restaurant for dinner." This time, she was mocking me, but I liked her honesty. Why do things you don't want to do, right?

It made me grin. She didn't turn me down. "Then I'll come to pick you up tonight." She nodded, keeping her eyes on the artwork-to-be.

"I'll be ready at eight" was all she said. I chuckled and shook my head, knowing exactly what spending time with her will be like in the future.

"Perfect. Eight. It's a date." I started walking back to the front door and couldn't help that stupid grin that seemed to become my new accessory because of Gray.

"There's still paint on your face!" she called out as I pushed open the door.

"I know," I responded, and I honestly did not care.

CHAPTER SEVEN

Gray

"I was hoping he wouldn't make a move this soon. We don't know that guy. What if he's just trying to have some fun and play stupid games with you? I don't need him to break your heart." I rolled my eyes at Dallas and shook my head. I lowered my head again, making sure all my brushes were clean before I put them away to dry. "So what if that happens? Dal, we've been through this before. I'm no longer a child. I'm old enough to make my own decisions and I won't listen to you when it comes to guys. Jagger is a nice guy and if I'm totally wrong about that, and if he really just tries to mess with me, then I'll learn from it."

He wasn't happy with my plan. His arms were crossed over his chest and the relaxed way he seemed to lean against the doorframe didn't look relaxed at all. "You're tensing up over nothing. Just let me handle this, okay? I'll go out with him, talk to him about this and that, and then I'll decide whether or not he will ever see me again. I'm not going to jump right into bed with him."

"I know that. It's just that you always said—" I interrupted him before he could say any more.

"I know what I said, Dallas. Just let me give him a try, all right?" I didn't need any more of his complaints and worries.

"Okay," he said, holding up his hands as a way to defend himself against my words. "But if he hurts you, I will have to do that shitty big brother move and beat him up. Just to be clear." I laughed it off, but I knew he was serious about it.

"Good. He did some underground fighting too."

"You think he's better than me?" he asked, his brows raised. I shrugged and put down the brushes to dry on the table. "I'm just saying that there are people who are stronger than you."

"That's not possible. I'm literally the best underground fighter in all North America. You were there and saw me win it all." He was proud of what he accomplished. At first, I wasn't sure fighting for money was a proud way to make money, but Dallas wouldn't do anything else. It's what he liked to do. And I wasn't going to interfere into his life.

"Do you hear that?" I asked with wide eyes, holding my hand up to my ear and leaning forward a bit.

"Hear what?" he asked, confused. My face fell, showing him how annoyed I was. "I think your arrogance just entered the building." And with that, I walked back to the front of the gallery, making sure all the lights were off. I heard Dallas chuckle and then follow me.

"Not sure why he would want to go on a date with you with that sense of humor you have. You're a real brat sometimes, you know that?" I knew he wasn't serious about that, but I did know that I sometimes tended to be a little too forward with my sarcasm.

I shrugged and grinned at him. "I guess he will have to live with that if he wants to get to know me better. Now, get out. He'll be here in half an hour and I still have to wipe the floor."

Dallas let out a small laugh and took out the keys from his pocket. "Let me know if you need anything." He squeezed my shoulder and then exited my gallery.

***

I heard the door open just twenty minutes later and I knew it was Jagger. Walking back to the front door, I saw him standing there with his hands shoved into his front pockets. His hair was combed back, and his outfit was, though all black, still classy. He looked handsome and I was surprised he put that much effort into it for a date with me.

"You do know I don't have anything else to change into," I told him, pointing at myself and my clothes.

Jagger looked down at my clothes and shrugged, then took a few more steps closer to pull me to him. I didn't mind him coming this close and touching me. I liked it. Every time he put his hand on my waist, I felt something inside of me. He bent his head and his lips pressed against my cheek, then he

47

smiled at me with that charming smile of his. "You look beautiful," he said, and I couldn't help but roll my eyes.

He chuckled, brushing a strand of hair out of my face. "What? You don't like compliments?" He kept staring into my eyes and didn't stop brushing back my hair behind my ear. I frowned and shook my head.

"Why not? I think you're beautiful no matter what you're wearing. I love seeing you in a big, oversized, paint-splotched sweater. Fits you perfectly. And those jeans," he stopped then and looked down at my legs. "Incredibly well-fitting," he said in a fascinated tone.

Just as I started questioning his weird, cringeworthy way of complimenting me, I realized he was mocking me. I scrunched up my nose and pushed against his chest. "Stop that. It's not funny," I told him and stepped away to grab my backpack, which was laying on the floor.

Jagger let out a laugh. "It is incredibly funny. You should see your face right now. I guess you're not the only one who's good at sarcasm."

"You're an asshole," I exclaimed but couldn't help a grin.

"What comes around, baby," he teased, his smile slowly fading. "But I don't mind if you're coming on a first date with me dressed as a painter. Actually...kinda hot. Not really into roleplay but...I'll handle it this one time." Again, he was joking.

This time I laughed, and I was starting to believe that there was no way this guy wasn't good. He was fun, yet he also had a calm, relaxed side to him. "If you don't stop that right now, I don't think it will take long for me to like you even more."

The corners of his mouth revealed a satisfied grin and I wondered if I should've said that. Because this time, I wasn't being sarcastic at all.

"You like me already?" he asked, wanting to hear me say it again.

I couldn't help but sigh and then I nodded, because hiding it now was too late. "Yes. You're a nice guy and I think you're fun. But I want to get to know you better. So, if this is just a little fling for you, let me know right now. I don't want to waste my time on that kinda stuff."

And there, I said it. Better now than never, right?

Jagger studied my face and I was unsure what he was thinking. He looked concerned, then surprised, but in the end, he smiled. "I guess you're lucky you met me then." He held out his hand for me to take and I first hesitated.

"That's not an answer, Jagger."

He nodded, then reached for my hand because I was still not putting mine in his. He pulled me closer, putting his other hand on my lower back and his face drew closer to mine. His lips pressed against my neck, taking a small nibble before he whispered against my skin: "I'm too old to be playing childish games like that, Rusty."

The use of my brother's nickname for me threw me off, and I couldn't help but laugh. "Idiot," I mumbled and pushed against his chest once again to get some distance between us. "Let's go," I said and started walking toward the door.

He wasn't even trying hard and I was already intrigued by him. After just two days of knowing him.

Damn him.

Damn you, Jagger Curtis.

CHAPTER EIGHT

Jagger

I was enjoying her company and by the looks she was giving me I knew she was happy to sit here with me too. Before picking her up, I made sure to ask Sage what Gray liked to eat. As her cousin and best friend, she was able to tell me exactly what Gray liked and which restaurant she goes to, so I made sure to make reservations for two at the Mexican place located near the city center. I also found out that Gray came here to celebrate her birthdays and that she loved the fact that every cocktail was free for the birthday girl and with the free cocktails came a huge sombrero to wear all evening. When I called to make the reservation, I was thinking about telling them that it was my birthday just to see what that buzz was all about. I didn't do that, though, thinking it would be a little too much for our first date.

"I gotta be honest," I told Gray, swallowing the last bite of my quesadilla. "This food is amazing,

51

and I think I'll come here again."

She let out a laugh and nodded, agreeing with my words. "I'll have to come here more often too. I usually just spend birthdays here." I knew that already, but I didn't want to interrupt her. "Sage doesn't like all the attention people in here give her when it's her birthday, but we come here anyway."

"And I thought Sage liked attention." I grinned.

"She does. But only attention from hot guys and friends who already know her."

I shrugged then, not wanting to spend more time talking about Sage. "Sounds weird to me."

Gray nodded, taking a sip from her iced margarita. "So, what's the story behind that scar?" she asked, pointing to the side of my face. I forgot about that scar from time to time. Since Dean's death, I tried not to think about him, and looking into a mirror and seeing that scar on my face brought back bad memories. I knew what I did wasn't right. Killing my father in front of my sister and her boyfriend was something I regretted deeply. But it had to be done and I knew Low was much calmer now.

I lifted my hand to touch the scar starting from below my left ear and down to the middle of the side of my neck and knew I couldn't tell her the truth. Telling her that my father tried to kill me when I was nine would scare her off. "After an underground fight, my opponent attacked me with a knife. It's not as bad as it looks," I lied. Perfect. Starting off good on our first date. And with that lie, I could've just told her the truth. *Jesus Christ.*

"It looks badass," she told me with a small grin.

"But that's horrible. I'm glad you're okay." I simply nodded and leaned back, studying her face.

"You once mentioned your sister and her boyfriend. What are they like?"

I smiled thinking about my family back in Hastings. "My sister, Harlow, she's a sweetheart. She's around your age and pregnant. I can't wait to meet that kid, honestly. I always knew she would find someone and start a family, but I never thought it would happen so fast. Hunter is her boyfriend. He's like a brother to me since we were teens and back then he was the biggest asshole I knew. I hated the thought of them being together and at the beginning, Hunter treated Low like shit. I hated him for that. But my sister's the type of person that still believes someone's a good person even when they've shown her a million times that they're not."

Gray was smiling at me and something close to fascination danced around her eyes. "She sounds like a wonderful person." I nodded and my smile grew wide. "She's the best damn person in my whole life. Our past wasn't easy but watching her go through hell and staying strong was incredible. I think you two would like each other. She needs a little crazy in her life."

"Are you calling me crazy?" Gray teased and I let out a laugh.

"I just think you two got different personalities and Low spends every day working and making sure her baby is growing healthy. Hunter never lets her leave the diner or the house unless Bliss convinces him."

"So, Bliss is her friend?" she then asked, and I

wondered if it was a mistake bringing up Bliss.

"Bliss is Hunter's sister," I explained and hoped that was enough.

Gray nodded. "I understand. Well, I would love to meet her someday."

"Actually, they're having a baby shower soon on Hunter's birthday. To find out the gender of the baby. I'm driving to Hastings and will probably stay there for a few days. Maybe you could join me."

Gray tilted her head to the side and studied my face. "Don't you think that's a little too soon to meet all your friends and family?" she asked. First, I didn't have many friends and family members in Hastings who would be attending that baby shower and second…"I've met your friends and some of your family members already."

"That's true. But won't your parents be around at your sister's gender reveal party?" That was a very good point if I did have any parents who actually were alive or knew their daughter was pregnant.

I simply shrugged. I couldn't tell her about the craziness going on with my parents. "It's in June. You still have time to think. It would be fun. Just let me know if you wanna join or not."

She nodded then, not trying to figure anything out. "I'll do that."

"Good. Would you like another margarita? You downed that one like an alcoholic," I joked and nodded to the empty glass in front of her.

She chuckled and shook her head. "No, thank you. I think it's time for us to go for a little walk and then head back home."

I agreed although I would've wanted to spend

some more time with her. I was enjoying her company, but I knew this wasn't our last date.

CHAPTER NINE

Jagger

After that Monday night I spent with Gray, we only texted now and then because of her working all week and not having much time to go out to eat with me again. She had promised me to come over to my apartment to eat dinner on Saturday, so I was looking forward to tomorrow.

I went grocery shopping this morning and made sure to also get a nice bottle of wine. Cooking wasn't something I did often. Back in Hastings, it was usually Harlow who did the cooking. Sometimes, when I was hungry late at night, I did warm up a can of Ravioli or prepared myself a bowl of salad, but that's where my skills with preparing meals ended. Not sure how I was going to convince Gray to eat anything I made. Calling up Hunter to ask him how to prepare a proper meal was probably my only option if I wanted Gray to keep seeing me after tomorrow night. That guy knew his way around a kitchen and I was glad Harlow got some real food in her system. From time to time, Low sends me pictures of meals Hunter prepared, and I would lie if I said that those pictures didn't make my mouth water.

I took one last glance into the fridge before closing it and sighing, wondering why I was so nervous to see her again. Gray. That beautiful and funny red-headed girl I only just met but made something in me want to get to know every little thing about her.

Normally, I wasn't the type of guy to be this intrigued by a girl. I never felt the urge to find love or to date. I never wanted to get to know someone romantically and never hoped for a relationship. Not even Bliss. But Bliss was different, and I knew that falling for someone in Hastings would never be an option. Too risky. People there talked too much. I knew dating any girl in Hastings would only cause problems. I saw the way I was looked at there and their eyes told me exactly what they thought of me. I was the outsider of the city. Just like Harlow and Hunter. Just like any other man or woman who lived on our side of town or the trailer park.

A knock on my door made me come back to reality. *Who could possibly be knocking on my door at almost nine p.m.?* I walked through the kitchen, passing the living room, and reaching the front door, opening it without looking through the peephole.

"You're alive!" Dallas exclaimed and grinned brightly, holding up a six-pack of beer.

"Huh?" I stepped aside as he welcomed himself inside, walking straight to my couch. Oh, well.

Some company might be nice.

"I've not seen you since the party. Thought something might've happened to you," he said, sitting down and opening one of the cans he brought. He leaned back and looked at me with a grin still on his face. "You okay, man?"

I snapped out of my trance and shook my head with a chuckle. "Yeah, sorry. I got some things on my mind." I walked over to the couch and sat down next to him. "Did you have a fight this week?" I asked, thinking it was a good topic to talk about. And by the looks of his knuckles I could tell he had recently hit something.

"Nah, just some training. My next fight is tomorrow night. You should come and bid on me. I can promise you'll win big." His face was serious now and I had no doubt that this guy wouldn't lose to anyone soon. I didn't follow all of his fights. There was a chart online for all the underground fights happening in the US, but I hadn't checked it in a while.

"Might come by. Who's the lucky guy?" I joked and he let out a laugh. "Kaleb Fury. Beat him four times already and I have no idea why he comes back and tries to beat me."

"Probably likes the pain." We both laughed and Dallas shrugged. "Maybe he'll realize after my fifth win that he's got no chance. Probably just likes the challenge."

I nodded in agreement. I'd been there before. Back when I started fighting, I had one opponent I was never able to win against. Since he was the best at the time, I wanted to be the one to break his lucky streak and take over his position of being the best fighter. Before I got the chance to challenge him again, that poor guy got knocked out by several men one night on the streets. They broke both his legs, damaging them to the point where he's not been able to fight anymore.

"You really don't fight anymore?" Dallas asked and turned to look at me. I shook my head and reached for a beer. "I think I'm over it. I fought to get money. Not sure I can just start fighting again after years of no practice."

"If you change your mind, you know where to find me. Do you work?" That was a reasonable question to ask someone who spent most of his time in his apartment. I shook my head and turned to look at him.

"Not yet. I haven't really found anything I like. I worked as a mechanic back in Hastings. But I think I need something different."

"I see. Ever thought about bartending? I always need people at the club."

I raised an eyebrow. "You own a club?"

"Yeah, a night club upstairs and a fight club downstairs," he explained with a smug grin. "I have a cave down there. And when I don't fight, I work upstairs at the bar sometimes. Only if my people don't have time to work. They're college students but most times they don't come in because of exams and all that shit. I usually don't hire people who work full-time. But since you don't have a job and you're not a student, I could get you a job at the bar."

That was…nice. I took a second to think about it

and to be honest, it didn't sound like a bad idea. Working as a bartender wasn't really what I had in mind when I started thinking about a new job, but Dallas is a nice guy. So why not just take this opportunity?

"Sounds good to me," I told him, and he gave me a quick nod.

"Great. I'll come get you tomorrow night at six and we can go to the club together so I can show you around before it opens at seven."

"That's not possible," I blurted out and hated myself for sounding harsh. Dallas looked at me with a surprised and then questioning look on his face. "What?"

"Your plan sounds good, but I have something planned already for tomorrow night. I can't cancel." Being honest was my only option here. "I have a date," I added slowly, hoping he would realize where I was going with that.

He studied me a while, then opened his mouth, closed it again, and then sighed. "My sister," he said, a little too annoyed for my liking. Shit. He's not okay with this.

"Listen, man," I started, running my hand through my hair, and thinking about how to explain it to him. "She's great—"

"Yeah, she is," he said with a laugh and shook his head. "You don't have to explain yourself. I never had to deal with a guy taking her out on a second date, but I have this weird thing inside of me telling me to make sure you're not an asshole."

So he knew about our first date. Why didn't he say anything about that? "I get it. Hell, my sister is having my best friend's baby back in Hastings. Believe me, I know what you're feeling right now. But I can promise you that Gray's not just someone I want to have fun with." That also didn't sound right, but I somehow needed to let him know that my intentions were good.

"I invited her to eat dinner with me here. I'll cook for her. Well, I'll at least try. But I really enjoy her company." I wasn't sure why I told him all that, but it just seemed right. I knew how he felt.

"Just don't mess with her."

I nodded, holding up my hands to defend myself from those words. "Not my plan."

Dallas went quiet for a while, finished his beer, and then grabbed another one. "Sunday, then. My fight starts at eight. We can go to the club at six, I show you around until seven, and then I'll get ready for my fight."

I nodded again, hoping he really accepted what I said before. "Sounds good to me. And, hey…if I mess it up with Gray, I'll let you beat me up."

Dallas laughed and shook his head. "You wouldn't want that."

Chapter Ten

Gray

I kept staring at the door. I couldn't get myself to knock on Jagger's door. I wasn't nervous. I never was. Especially not when it came to guys. They didn't make me nervous. Not one bit. But something about Jagger made me feel weird inside. I liked him. A lot. We had an amazing date and we even got closer with his hand on my thigh or his arm around my shoulders as he walked me home. It didn't bother me on our first date. I felt comfortable around him and I wasn't going to push him away. He obviously liked me. He even told me. He was a gentleman, holding the doors for me and paying for the food.

He didn't hold back on touching me. It might be weird for some people to let a stranger you only just met a few days prior touch you, but Jagger did it in such a gentle, unobtrusive way that I wanted his hand to stay there all evening.

The way he talked, so calm and yet determined,

he knew what he wanted to say and picked his words carefully. He looked relaxed, as if we did that so many times already. He listened. He was patient with me and my messy way to tell stories. I was all over the place. But he kept his eyes on mine, nodded occasionally to let me know that he was following what I was saying. And the way he kept our conversation flowing without even trying too hard. He knew what he wanted to ask. What he wanted to know about me. And in general, how to keep a conversation going without it getting boring or one-sided.

I think I did well myself. I answered his questions and asked back when I wanted to know something about him. He was honest with me. He was genuine.

Too genuine.

Which is why I was hesitant to knock on his door. He seemed unreal. Too good to be true. *How am I supposed to keep up with someone like him?*

No. I'm worth this. I deserve a nice guy.

Shaking my head, I pulled myself together and finally lifted my hand to knock. Two knocks. My heart made itself noticeable in my chest now. *Great. I take it back. I am nervous.*

The door opened, and I held my breath as my eyes wandered from his brown chino pants up to his plain navy sweater, nicely fitting his upper body. Not too tight, but snug enough to see a little bit of his muscles. The sleeves were nicely rolled halfway up his arms. My eyes met his and smiles immediately spread on our faces.

"You look handsome," I told him, eyeing his hair

for a second. It was a little messy, with two or three locks curling around his ears, giving the whole look the finishing touch.

He chuckled and stepped forward, grabbed my waist with his right hand, cupped the side of my face with his left. He kissed my cheek softly and I closed my eyes to make sure I would remember this forever. The way he pulled me in, the way he kissed me, so gentle—that's what I liked about him. He got close without making me feel uncomfortable. And he wasn't making this awkward.

He then stepped back again to look at me. "You're beautiful." His eyes were now wandering over my outfit. I was wearing an olive-green cord skirt with a white long-sleeved turtleneck. Nothing too fancy. I wanted to still be comfortable.

When his eyes met mine again, he stepped aside and nodded inside. "Come in. Dinner's almost ready."

"Thanks." I walked inside the apartment and was immediately greeted by the smell of something I couldn't identify. A mixture of spices and freshly chopped herbs.

"What are you cooking?" I asked, putting down the tote bag I probably shouldn't have taken on a date since it was old and grungy. But I didn't have a purse at home and a backpack seemed a little unnecessary. I pulled out the bottle of red wine I had bought some weeks ago to consume on my own but never actually had the chance to and turned to look at him. "I hope whatever it is goes with cheap red wine." I grinned, holding out the bottle to him.

He chuckled, amused by my attempt at making

cheap wine sound tempting. He took the bottle and looked at the label, then nodded. "I think this will go perfectly with what I'm cooking. Come with me," he said with a smile and walked into the open kitchen. I followed him, watching him open a drawer and pull out a corkscrew.

I glanced over to the counter, noticing a variety of vegetables, some salad, and different bowls with sauces in them. Then I saw buns sitting on an oven tray, and it all started to click. "You're making burgers?" I asked, getting my hopes up.

"*We* are making burgers," he explained and pulled the cork out of the bottle swiftly. "I know it's not a nice steak, but to be honest with you...I could never pull off anything other than home-made burgers. Or some frozen pizza." He looked as if he was doubting himself, looking over at the little buffet he put together on the kitchen counter. I glanced back at it too, then let out a laugh and shook my head to let him know that I was totally into this.

"This is amazing. It's a great idea, Jagger." I smiled brightly at him, feeling an urge to hug him tight.

He seemed relieved, visibly relaxing the muscles in his face again. "I'm glad you like it. I had to call Hunter and ask about that special sauce he makes for the diner. That's his recipe." He poured the wine into two glasses and handed one to me.

"I bet it tastes great. Thank you for this," I told him and nodded to the buffet. I took the glass from him and held it up to his, so our glasses clinked. "And for asking me out on a second date."

He grinned, holding his glass up to his mouth and taking a sip. "Wasn't the last time I'll ask you out."

I hoped so. We hadn't even started dinner yet, but I knew I didn't want to leave his place. Not tonight.

Chapter Eleven

Jagger

She liked the burgers. She told me multiple times while we sat at the table and enjoyed our creations. Gray liked Hunter's sauce, and I was thankful he sent me that recipe. I liked it too. But then, I already knew what that sauce would taste like. I enjoyed Hunter's cooking skills back in Hastings, and after eating these burgers, I sure as hell would drive over there and eat at Frankie's diner.

"The third one was a mistake," Gray admitted and sat down on the couch. I grinned, taking both our wine glasses and putting them down on the small table in front of her. I sat down next to her and leaned back, stretching one arm behind her on the back of the couch. "I think it's impressive how much you can eat. But I agree. Three burgers are a lot. I'm full too."

After we cleaned the table and put the dishes into the dishwasher, sitting on the couch with her and drinking wine was all I wanted to do for the rest of the evening. Having her here with me was nice. Her presence was somehow calming but exciting and talking to her was easy.

"How's work?" I asked, eyeing her face once again. I seemed to do that a little too often but then, she was fascinating. How could I look away?

"Work's great. I finished the painting I started when you came to the gallery, and now, I'm brainstorming on what to paint next." Her eyes left mine and wandered around my apartment, then the corners of her mouth turned up. "Maybe I could do one for your place. It does look a bit plain."

"I agree," I told her and smiled back, reaching to my glass of wine, and taking a sip. "What do you think would fit in here? More color, or should I keep it minimalistic and neutral?" That was a question I couldn't answer myself because my sense of color and interior design was nowhere to be found. Besides, this place was too big for just one person and the emptiness in the guest bedroom was sad. I kept that door closed, so I didn't have to think about buying a bed no one would ever use. Unless Harlow and Hunter would come over one day. Looking for a roommate was not an option. I liked being alone and falling asleep at night without hearing someone going to the bathroom or waking up too early and making noise when I still had time to rest.

It wasn't a problem with Harlow since she's the calmest and most attentive girl ever. She did wake up before me most mornings, but she was so careful not to make any noise so that I was able to sleep off the long nights I had most times. Also, back then I was the one waking up in the middle of the night from Hunter or Gunner's calls. I had to meet them in the middle of the night, making sure our job was done before sunrise. It was hectic and wrong. I realized that working for Gunner wasn't getting me anywhere and I had to change for Harlow. After all that happened with our dad, I needed a way out. Luckily, Hunter stood right next to me through all of it and telling Gunner we would be leaving his business was easier together than doing it all alone.

"I think some neutrals fit perfectly." Gray's voice made me snap out of my thoughts, and I saw her look around the room once again. "I like the dark floor in here and the black frames on the windows. Plants would also look great in here. So maybe...a painting with browns and greens?"

I quickly nodded, thinking whatever she thought would look good in here, I was okay with. "Sounds perfect," I agreed, putting the wine glass back on the couch table. "Anything else you think would fit in this space?"

Gray studied the furniture around the living room, puckering her lips to let me know that she was thinking. "Other than some plants, I think this place looks great. It's simple and cozy. And I love that there are no curtains in front of the windows. Sage has them all over her apartment and I think it blocks out too much of the sun." She turned to look at me again with a smile. "I like your place a lot better."

And I liked having her in it. Fuck me. Resisting the urge to pull her in and kiss her was hard. I didn't want to mess this up. But I couldn't wait to have her just a little closer tonight.

Our eyes stayed on each other's for a while, then, I reached for her leg and pulled it over my lap. "Come here," I told her in a low voice, and she moved closer, leaning into me, and laying her head on my shoulder. My right hand cupped the back of her head and my fingers moved into her hair, caressing her scalp.

Her left arm wrapped around my waist from the back, and her right hand gripped my sweater, holding tightly to me. I turned my head to rest my chin on the top of her head, inhaling her scent, which reminded me of peaches with a hint of honey. *Interesting mix*, I thought. *Just what I like*.

We stayed like that for a while, not caring about the time passing. It was getting late. We spent most of our evening talking at the table and eating. So now, sitting here in silence felt just right. I liked how we didn't bother talking, yet we knew exactly what we were feeling and thinking. With Gray, enjoying each other even without saying a word was a big step for me. For example, I didn't like the pressure Bliss put on me. When she was around, we talked a lot. And as soon as it got quiet for a few minutes, she got mad because, in her eyes, the silence meant that something was wrong. That's how most of our fights started. Her thinking something was up just because I didn't talk for a while. I couldn't stand those moments. But this, with Gray, this was already feeling good.

Her fingers traced up my sweater to my chest, and then back down to my stomach, where she gripped the fabric tightly again. "I'm sleepy," she whispered, and I turned to kiss the top of her head. I didn't want her to leave. I wanted to wake up the next morning and have her here with me. In my apartment. So, I risked it.

"You can stay here. I'll sleep on the couch."

"Okay," she responded with no hesitation. A grin appeared on my lips, and I grabbed a fistful of her hair to turn her head enough so I could kiss her forehead softly. "I'll show you my room."

I took her hand in mine as we got up from the couch and walked toward the bedroom. I led her inside and turned on the lights, then nodded to my clothing rack where all my stuff was hung. "Just take whatever you need. The bathroom is right there," I said with another nod to the bathroom door located opposite the bed. "There's a cabinet with some unused toothbrushes."

"Okay, thank you," she replied, then looked up to me with a small smile. "Will you be okay on the couch?" Her hand was still holding mine, with her fingers now linked with mine.

"I'll be just fine. Don't worry about me."

"All right, then…goodnight." I couldn't help a smile. She was so damn adorable. I squeezed her hand, then let go of it.

"Goodnight," I said, and she closed the door to my room.

I walked back to the couch, grabbing the pillows from one side and a blanket from the other. I fell asleep on here before. Wasn't that bad. But knowing Gray was right there in my bedroom was difficult to get ahold of. No need to rush things with her, though, right?

CHAPTER TWELVE

Gray

I couldn't sleep. Knowing Jagger was out there on the couch when this bed was big enough for three people didn't seem right. Besides, it's his bed. I should be the one to sleep on the couch. The evening we spent together was amazing. His company was, once again, very enjoyable. We had so much to talk about and the food...God, those burgers were delicious. I had to thank his friend for letting Jagger use his recipe one day. And I most definitely needed to drive to Hastings just to eat at that diner.

Then, the way he held me on the couch, so careful yet determined to keep me close. This man. Not sure how any other guy would ever be able to make me feel better than he can. I felt safe in his arms, even though we only just met a few days ago.

Letting him sleep out there didn't feel right at all. That's why I was sitting in his bed, contemplating whether to get up and ask him if he wants to join me in his bedroom. Just a small, kind gesture, right?

I stared at the door a while longer, then finally decided to get up. I walked over, opened the door slowly, hoping he wasn't asleep yet. As I stepped outside the bedroom, I saw Jagger sitting on the couch with just a shirt and boxers on, and a book in his hand. *Of course, he reads.* I almost rolled my eyes. Could he get any sexier?

He looked up, noticing me standing there in the hallway. His eyes moved from my face down my body, seeing that I had one of his sweaters on which just covered my bottom. Silence. We were getting good at silence. I liked it when we sat on the couch after dinner. It was nice knowing there were no words needed at times.

But I had to speak to let him know what I wanted. "I'd like you to come to bed." My voice was soft yet demanding. Not sure why I felt the need to tell him what to do in his own home but letting him know what I wanted was important. I didn't like miscommunications, and by being straight forward, I would avoid them.

Jagger put his book down on the couch next to him, then stood up and walked toward me slowly. I watched him carefully, and when he stopped in front of me, I smiled. Close. That's what I wanted him to be.

He was still silent, and with one more look at the sweater I had on, he reached up to tug my hair behind my ear. "I don't think I will be able to keep my hands off you if we lay in the same bed." His voice was husky and low, and his hand was now on my hip, already confirming that he would not keep them off me.

"Maybe that's exactly what I want," I teased. Our eyes met again, but his soon dropped to my lips, a grin appearing on his face. Now, all that was left to do was make the next move. And I thought, *if I started this, I could continue it*. So, I did.

I moved closer, put one of my hands on his chest and the other on the side of his neck, leaned in, and met his lips halfway. His hands soon were on my body, one holding me close to him on my lower back and the other gripping my hair at the back of my head. His lips were soft, and they moved gently over mine. I had no doubt they would feel this good.

Jagger moved, pushing me back against the wall right next to his bedroom door. His body leaned in against mine and I pulled him closer, so I was able to deepen the kiss. Our lips parted more, and I felt his tongue against mine immediately. He sure knew how to kiss. His rhythm was just right and the way his hands held my body made me shiver all over again. But then, his hands were one of the main things I liked about him. He knew how to use them. He knew what felt good when he touched me. But that also meant he had a lot of experience.

No, I'm not going there. What he had in the past with other women is not my business.

His right hand moved back to my hip, then slowly made its way to the side of my thigh, lifting the hem of his sweater and pushing his hand under it so he was able to touch my skin. His hand was warm, and the tenderness with which he touched me was perfect. When his hand moved up to my waist, his other hand reached behind me to cover my bottom. Right where I wanted it.

My hands made their way up to his neck, gripping and tugging on his hair lightly. He had nice hair. Full locks. Just how I liked it.

His knee pushed between my legs, seconds later he pulled me up by my bottom and I wrapped myself around his hips, feeling his hardness right at my center. He stepped away from the wall, carrying me into his bedroom without his lips leaving mine. He stopped at the end of the bed, putting one knee on it, and lowering me back onto the mattress, following me and still not breaking our kiss. The word passionate was too weak to describe our situation. He leaned over me, one hand gripping my neck to deepen the kiss even more and pushing his tongue further into my mouth. God, it felt so good.

My sweater was pushed up, exposing my belly. He was holding himself up with his left hand, but still let his body push down on mine with my legs up against his sides. "Tell me what you want, Gray," he mumbled against my lips and I quickly touched the waistband of his boxers. Instinctively, I grabbed for what I wanted to come off. But I wasn't sure going that far was necessary just now. This was our second date. Although sleeping with Jagger sounded exciting, I didn't think it was the best thing to do. There was an obvious attraction between the two of us, but I liked us back on that couch, just holding each other, becoming close without using too many words. Kissing him was also enough for now. Even if my body told me a whole other story.

Moving too quickly when dating someone never ended well for me. I got bored easily, and I wanted to take my time with Jagger. As much as possible. I wanted to get to know him. So, him asking what I wanted was perfect. He had enough respect toward me to find out what I wanted, other than just pushing us in a direction we both might regret sooner or later.

"I want you to hold me again," I whispered against his lips, taking my hand off his waistband and touching his stomach instead. He looked down into my eyes, the tip of his nose touching mine. He smiled, then moved his hand from my neck to my waist, pulling down the sweater to cover me back up. Jagger then moved to the side, adjusting the pillow behind his head, and laying back against it.

"Come here." He opened his arms, offering me the spot between them. Without hesitation, I moved closer into his embrace and nestled my face into the crook of his neck.

"You okay?" His voice was low and had a hint of concern in it. I nodded and gripped his shirt tightly, just like I did on the couch before. Something made me want to hold on to him. I felt safe with him. Protected. But I wasn't sure if he only acted that way to make people feel good and fall for his charms. *No, that sounds wrong,* I thought, *he's not that kind of guy.*

"I've never been better," I told him.

I felt his chest vibrate and heard a low chuckle escape him. "Fuck me," he mumbled, then pressed a kiss to my head and put his hand on top of mine. "You're too damn sweet."

CHAPTER THIRTEEN

Jagger

The last time I woke up with a girl next to me, Bliss was still coming around. Well, it hasn't been that long since she last came by, but I didn't want to compare Bliss with Gray. It felt different. Probably because Gray wasn't an old friend I've known for almost all my life. This was new. And better. So much better.

My arms were still around Gray, keeping her close to my body and feeling her warmth. The sun was shining through the big window, and I kept my eyes closed, enjoying how the rays felt on my face. For the first time in weeks, hell, even months, waking up in this bed felt right.

Gray's breathing was slow, and I could barely hear it. How was it possible that even in her sleep, without trying, she was being adorable? It fascinated me how calm she was. And that might've been why I was feeling safe and relaxed next to her. She reminded me of Harlow in a way.

My sister had a way of pulling me down to earth every time I was high on adrenaline or stressed from work. The moment I opened the front door and heard Harlow's sweet voice greet me, I was safe. She often told me I was her safe place. But she had no idea that I felt the same way about her. I often held her close on the couch, stroking her hair and waiting until she fell asleep with her head on my shoulder. She needed it. She had no other person in her life who would comfort her when she had a rough day at work. Well, until Hunter came around.

With Gray, I wondered if I would ever become what Hunter is for Harlow. Even if it was too early to tell, I knew I wanted to keep her close.

I moved my hand up her back, then gripped the back of her neck and turned my head to kiss her forehead, my eyes still closed. She moved in my arms, then a noise escaped her.

"Morning," she mumbled, and I now looked down at her. She had a small smile on her face, and a chunk of her hair was blocking my view. I moved it behind her ear and kissed her forehead once more before replying.

"Good morning. Sleep well?" I asked.

She nodded, then finally opened her eyes to look up into mine. She was gorgeous. "You?"

"Me too. I'm glad you let me come sleep here in my bed with you."

She laughed and pulled the covers up to her chin, then closed her eyes again. "I'm glad I let you too." A chuckle escaped me, and I started massaging the back of her head, and with the other hand I grabbed her hand, which was laying on my chest.

"Are you hungry? I can make us some pancakes," I asked, looking out the window and squinting at the sun. I can't remember the last time I've seen rain.

"Sounds good." She moved again and I felt her lips pressing against my jawline. "I'll go take a shower."

I watched her pick up her clothes from the floor and walk into the bathroom. I couldn't help but look at her barely covered bottom. I liked my sweater on her. A lot.

My hands moved into my hair, and I stayed in bed for a minute before getting up myself and walking out to the kitchen to make sure I had what was needed for pancakes. Of course, I didn't have any eggs. Great. I should be prepared for situations like this next time.

I looked at the clock on the wall and decided that it wasn't too early to go upstairs and ask Sage if she had any eggs for me to borrow. With a glance to my bedroom, I walked to the bathroom door. "Hey, Gray?" I called out and knocked on the door twice. "I'll go ask Sage if she has some eggs. I'm out."

"Okay! Tell her I said hi," came from the bathroom and the shower turned on. Perfect. So, she didn't feel weird about her cousin knowing that she was here with me. I smiled at the thought of that and made my way back to the kitchen. I quickly googled how many eggs I needed for the pancakes and rolled my eyes when I saw that I would only need one. But the recipe said it's "The best pancake recipe ever," so I wasn't going to mess it up. I needed that egg.

I put on a pair of sneakers to walk upstairs to Sage's apartment and knocked on her door. Just seconds later, she opened the door with a big frown on her face and a robe around her body. "Don't tell me she left already," Sage warned and crossed her arms over her chest.

"What? No…she's taking a shower." I wasn't really surprised that she knew about Gray being at my place. Gray must've told her. "I need to borrow an egg. I wanna make pancakes for her."

"Good choice. She likes pancakes." Sage walked back into the apartment and kept talking. "I'm glad she stayed overnight. She really needed that."

I raised a brow and leaned against the doorframe. "Really needed what?" I asked, watching as she walked back toward me with an egg in her hand. She imitated my facial expression and laughed.

"Sex. She needed to finally come out of that shell of hers. She's been tense for months. I'm glad you two finally did it. She's not been with a guy in so damn long."

Normally, if Gray and I having sex was the case, I would be annoyed by Sage's words. But knowing Gray, even for this short amount of time, I knew sex wasn't what she was looking for. She was the one who stopped it last night, and I was glad she did. If she wouldn't have, I probably couldn't have stopped myself from stripping her naked to feel my cock inside her.

Christ, Jag.

I wasn't sure if I should tell Sage that we didn't have sex—just to make sure she wasn't interpreting anything into what Gray and I had. But then, I didn't like people playing a part in my personal life. Not when it came to girls. It's not like I walked around Hastings and told everyone about Bliss and me. So, I decided to let it slip.

I reached for the egg and smiled. "Thanks for this," I told her and stepped away from the door again. "See you around." And with one last nod, I turned to walk back down to my apartment. As I entered it, I saw Gray standing in the kitchen with her wet hair up in a bun at the top of her head and an orange in her hand. She turned to look at me and smiled.

"Mind if I make some orange juice?" she asked, holding the orange up.

"Go ahead," I said and walked over to her, put my hand on her lower back and kissed her cheek, close to the corner of her mouth. "You feeling good today?"

She looked up into my eyes with a soft smile and nodded. "Very." Then her lips pressed into a thin line and a small crease appeared between her brows. She suddenly looked conflicted, which made me chuckle.

"What's wrong?"

She kept frowning at me, and I couldn't help but grin. She was studying my face and I was waiting on her to answer. "Is it okay if I get used to this already? I mean, waking up in your bed and making breakfast with you?"

I glanced down at her, eyeing the turtleneck and skirt she wore to our date last night. I puckered my lips, looking back into her eyes. "Only if you promise me that next time, you'll leave on my sweater." I wanted to see a little more of her legs. The skirt she was wearing was short, but I liked the teasing of her ass peeking out from under the sweater.

Her face relaxed slowly, and a smile appeared on her lips. She nodded, moved closer to me, and kissed me quickly on the lips. "Deal." Then she turned back to the counter and started cutting the oranges in half. I let out a chuckle once again, then shook my head and turned to find the other ingredients needed for the pancakes.

She felt comfortable around me and Gray's words contradicted what Sage told me. She wasn't here just to get her frustration out. She was here for me. To get to know me and spend time with me. And I was happy that's why she was with me. I was starting to get used to her too. Slowly, but very surely.

CHAPTER FOURTEEN

Gray

"Are you full?" Jagger asked, nodding to my clean plate. I had enough pancakes and the burgers from last night were still taking up a lot of space in my stomach. I nodded and put my hands on my belly. "Very full. Thank you."

Jagger smiled and leaned back in his seat, studying my face once again. He did that a lot lately. And I didn't mind. Although his eyes were hard to read, I could tell he was satisfied, so I kept my eyes on his face too. "What are you up to today?" I asked, pulling one knee up and resting my chin on it.

"Your brother offered me a job at his club. He's picking me up at six." I couldn't help but roll my eyes. "What? You don't like the idea of me working for your brother?" he asked with a grin and a tilt of his head.

"No, that's not it. I somehow knew it would happen." I puckered my lips, then smiled at him softly. "Dallas told me about your fighting career years back. He knows I don't like what he's doing. It's stupid and dangerous."

Jagger nodded, seemingly agreeing with me on that. "It is stupid and dangerous. But it's also very calming in a way. Well, at least for me it was." He shrugged, letting me know that my opinion on fighting didn't matter. It didn't. I just hoped Dallas would stop with it.

"Why did you fight?" I asked him, hoping to get a little backstory on it. Some people did have a reason to fight. Dallas just did it for fun and because he somehow became kind of famous. He was good, I'd give him that. But his reasons for beating up other guys for money were weak.

"I started when I was young. Fourteen or fifteen. I was struggling with some family stuff and needed a way to get my anger out. And since my parents didn't have any money to take good care of me and my sister, fighting became the only way to help at home, and give Low a better childhood. I sucked when I first started, but I kept training. Turned out I was secretly the crowd's favorite. Then, when I moved town, I stopped. I had enough of broken noses and bruises all over my body."

"So…what did you do then?" His story was somehow dark but sweet. He took on all the beatings from strangers so his family could have a better life. That's a good reason. Dallas just did it to be the greatest. Selfish. I still loved him, but I hated seeing him hurt.

"I found a job as a mechanic. Turned out I was good at fixing cars and motorcycles. And it was fun.

Harlow didn't approve of the fighting, anyway. I didn't want her to worry anymore."

I smiled at his words. Harlow's lucky. Having a big brother like Jagger must be nice. Not that I don't think Dallas is a good brother, but he has that annoying big brother thing. Always trying to act like my protector but getting on my nerves most of the time.

"Speaking of Harlow," I said with a nod to his phone right next to his plate. It lit up once, then twice, with her name written on the screen. Jagger looked down and read what his sister texted. A sigh escaped him, and I couldn't help but be curious.

"Something wrong?" I wondered, keeping my eyes on him.

***

Jagger

I stared at Harlow's text for some seconds before looking up at Gray again. "No, nothing's wrong," I assured her and smiled. "Before I came to Newton, I let Hunter move into my home with Harlow but I'm still the owner. She needs me to sign some papers so they can be set as owners. I could ask her to send me the papers, but she wouldn't do that. I need to go back to Hastings for a few days. Make sure she's not freaking out about me not visiting her in a while."

Gray nodded but didn't say a word, seemingly thinking about something. I kept my eyes on hers, knowing she was about to propose something I may or may not regret agreeing to. "Would you like some company for the long ride?"

A grin appeared on my face because that's exactly what I expected her to ask. I knew taking her with me to Hastings was a big step. First, she would be meeting the two people who were closest to me, and second...Bliss was there. Hunter told me about Bliss and Harlow hanging out more often, and there was no way around her when I went back to visit my sister. But then, if Gray was with me, and Bliss saw how close we had gotten, she might finally let go of her obsession over me.

"Are you sure you wanna drive three and a half hours to Hastings with me, just for me to sign some papers?" I wasn't going to stop her from doing just that, because I did want her with me. I was just making sure she was certain of her own plan.

She shrugged, giving me a shy smile. "Your sister sounds nice. And you said Frankie's Diner is incredible. So...yes. I do want to drive three and a half hours down to Hastings with you."

I laughed, getting up from my seat and takin a step to her. I leaned down, cupping her face in my hand, and kissing her lips. I was getting a little too comfortable with this. Kissing and touching her whenever I wanted to. But she didn't seem to mind. Her lips moved gently against mine and a small moan escaped her throat. Fuck. She didn't seem to mind at all.

I moved away from her again and grabbed my phone. "Which days work best for you?" I asked Gray, making sure I wouldn't just pick a day myself. I would have to let Dallas know about it tonight if I decided to start working at his club after tonight.

"I can close the gallery from Tuesday to Thursday. Not many customers coming in on those days," she explained and got up from the table and started putting away the dishes. I nodded and typed a message for Harlow, letting her know that I would be driving to Hastings on Tuesday and staying a few days. I included my companion's name.

"Great. Tuesday through Thursday, then." I put my phone on the counter and helped her clean up the table.

I was excited for Gray to meet Harlow. I was sure they would get along well. Hunter might joke around with me, telling me that he saw this coming. And Bliss...let's just say I wished she wouldn't start a scene the moment she saw Gray.

CHAPTER FIFTEEN

Jagger

Later that day, Gray left after giving me another one of her sweet kisses and a bright smile, telling me how excited she was to drive up down to Hastings and meeting my family and friends. I was excited too. First, because of the long drive ahead of us, and second, because I would see Harlow again. I missed her a lot, even though I was the one dragging my heels to go see her. There was always someone standing in my way to go back. But now, it seemed like I could step in front of that person without any worries that something would happen between us. I was over her a long time ago, but sex did sound appealing with her.

With Gray too. But since my heart didn't feel like breaking hers, I wouldn't push her too far. I wanted her to come to me. Tell me what she wanted. How she wanted it.

While I was fantasizing about Gray and where we were heading, her brother opened my front door unannounced and stepped into my apartment without permission once again. I looked up from the sandwich I was eating and leaned back against the counter.

"I should lock that door," I mumbled, keeping my eyes on him, and raising an eyebrow, silently asking what his deal was with trespassing.

"Are you ready? What...you look like you've had a rough day." His words were amused, which did not reflect my facial expression. How was he so annoying, but at the same time acceptably fun to be around? That was controversial as fuck, but somehow he pulled it off.

"I was just thinking about getting a restraining order against you, so you'd stop coming in my apartment without asking for permission." I was joking, of course. But it was a little annoying. What if Gray was still here and we were still making out right here in the kitchen, with me standing between her legs while they were holding me tightly against her body?

Dallas laughed and walked right up to my fridge, opening it, and taking out a can of Coke. "If you do that, I'll make sure Gray doesn't step into your apartment, either. I saw her leave earlier. She had a big fucking grin on her face."

I smiled at that because we had a great night last night and this morning was nice too. "We get along pretty well. She's amazing," I told him and took a bite of my sandwich. He nodded, opening the can, and taking a long sip. As he drank, he kept his eyes on me. Concern flashed through them, and I knew he was trying to figure out if he should just let go of it and accept that I was dating his sister now. I was good at reading people. I've read Harlow's thoughts since she was little. But then, finding out what she was thinking wasn't hard. Her eyes told stories. One look at her, and you immediately knew how she felt. But that was also because she wanted people to be able to read her when words didn't come to her easily.

Dallas was different. He tried to hide his thoughts, but that didn't work with me. "I've told you before, man. I have good intentions with Gray. I like her." I hoped that was enough to ease his mind. He studied me for a while, then nodded and chugged the whole can. "Let's see how well you do tonight. If you can work the bar right, I'll let you see my sister again. If you mess up, I get to fight you and then kick out of this town."

I laughed hard at his stupidly crazy imagination and finished my sandwich. "Watch it, Washington. Just because I stopped fighting doesn't mean I'm not good at it."

"We'll see. Come on. We gotta go."

***

The club Dallas owned was called *The Red*. Not sure if the name was as boring as it sounded, or if I just had higher expectations for a fight club. But then, people who didn't come to the club for alcohol and parties probably didn't know there was underground fighting going on. Because then, the name *The Red* made some sense, since the floor where the fights took place was painted red.

We immediately went down to the fighting space as we entered the back entrance to the club. Dallas told me he wanted to show me where he had his fights, and probably just wanted to show off his cage. It was big, I'd give him that. But it was too clean. The club I fought at had broken down walls and bloodstains on the floor no one cared to clean after fights. His club didn't fit the underground fights stereotypes.

"You have a fight tonight, right?" I asked and looked over at him. He nodded, gleaming at the slightly elevated cage. He was proud of it. And proud of fighting in it too. "Yeah, I'll let you come watch if you want. I think I got enough guys upstairs tonight so you can come bet on me." His grin grew and I chuckled. "I'm not spending my money on stupid shit like this anymore. But I'd love to watch you get punched in the face. I had this urge in me to do it myself before we came here, but I need the job."

I was being sarcastic and luckily, Dallas didn't take anything I said seriously. He laughed it off and nodded toward two doors right next to the staircase we came from. "Those are the changing rooms. And over there are some bathrooms." He then pointed to the other two doors on the other side of the stairs. I nodded, not sure about why he told me all of that. It's not like I intended on fighting here.

"Let's go upstairs. I'll show you some things and then let Levi take over. He's a good friend of mine and actually owned the club before I did," Dallas explained and started walking back to the stairs. I followed him, taking one last look at the cage. *It does look appealing. No, no more fights.*

"Did Levi fight too?"

"Yeah, but he had to stop a few years ago because of his injuries. He's a badass. Don't fuck with him. He's got more muscles than both of us together."

"Got it."

As we got to the top and entered the night club area, my eyes immediately flew to the two strip poles in the middle of the floor. I raised an eyebrow, wondering if I missed something when Dallas first talked about his club.

"You're not the owner of a strip club, right?"

That made Dallas chuckle. "No, but we have some girls coming around to put on a show every time I have a fight down there. It pulls customers. Male, horny, old customers who happen to have fat wallets too."

I nodded slowly, thinking that it wasn't a bad idea to hire some strippers to get more people to watch your fight. Smart strategy, I'll give him that.

Dallas showed me around the club, explaining some things here and there and showing me all the important rooms that I needed to know about before starting at the bar. When we made our way back to the bar, a big guy walked through the doors which led to the kitchen, holding a case of beer in his hand. He put it down on the counter and looked at us, then nodded. "This your friend?" he asked Dallas.

"Yeah, this is Jagger Curtis. Can you show him around the bar and kitchen? Show him how to make some drinks and all that stuff. I'm gonna get ready."

Levi nodded and held out his hand for me to take, and I did, shaking it once and letting go of it again.

"Levi. Follow me. I'll show you where we store our bottles in case they go out. Tonight's a big night."

I didn't doubt that. Dallas Washington's fights were always a big deal. And I was excited to see him fight tonight.

Chapter Sixteen

Gray

"I don't think it's a good idea that I'm here, Sage." I crossed my arms over my chest and looked up at the club's sign. Sage made me dress up and come here for reasons that would only benefit her. Joey would be here to watch my brother's fight, and Sage liked to party. I knew about Dallas's fights and how many people came to see them, but I had no interest in watching him beat the shit out of another guy. I also had no interest in sitting in a booth upstairs and watching others drink themselves into a coma or dance like crazy people.

Or maybe I just didn't want to be that crazy girl stalking the guy she's dating and following him around town like a puppy. I knew about Jagger getting a job at The Red because he told me. He wanted to make sure I was okay with him working close to my brother. I didn't mind. But I didn't want to come off as clingy.

"Nothing I ever drag you to seems to be a good

idea to you. Come on, it will be fun." She pulled me toward the entrance where Andrew was standing. He's a huge guy, making sure only people who are old enough to enter get inside the club. "Girls," he said with a nod and stepped aside for us to get in.

"Hi, Andrew," I greeted him with a small smile, appreciating the way he stopped checking our ID's since Dallas told him to just let us in. *You are family*, Dallas always said, *you're always welcome at the club*.

Sage took that for granted. She spent most nights here after work and hung out with Joey and his college friends. But the last time I was here, I almost had a heart attack watching Dallas fight some guy who obviously was much weaker than him. I left early that night, ignoring all the men watching those strippers on the poles. Let's just say that The Red was not my scene. Eating snacks and watching movies was more my speed.

"Joey is already here," Sage informed me and pointed to a booth her boyfriend was sitting in. "He told me his friends won't be around until the fight starts. But he's got some beer for us. Come on." That didn't really appeal to me. Not much did in here. The only thing I found intriguing was the brown-haired and incredibly handsome guy standing behind the bar, smiling my direction. Jagger seemed surprised but pleased to see me. I smiled back, hoping he didn't see this as me stalking him. We'd seen each other some hours ago, and I still couldn't get the way his lips tasted out of my head.

"I'll be right there," I told Sage and walked over

the dancefloor to get to the bar. Not many people were ordering drinks. As soon as I got there, Jagger's smile turned into a smirk.

"Here to see me?" he mocked, and I couldn't help a laugh.

"Sage dragged me here. I told her it would be weird if I just showed up at your job after our first night together." I reached for the peanuts on the counter and put them into my mouth with an apologetic smile.

Jagger chuckled and shook his head. "It's your brother's club and he's got a fight tonight. I'm happy to see you again." He said the last part with such honesty in his voice that it made my heart flutter.

"I'm happy to see you too," I told him sincerely, wishing I could go behind the bar to hug him. But keeping my distance was the better thing to do. He was still working, and I had no reason to distract him.

"So…did you ask Dallas about next week yet?"

"Uh, no. Didn't get the chance to. But I will, don't worry." His smile appeared again, and I nodded.

"Let me go ask him. He might take it better that way," I offered. "By the way, you look good behind this bar. Suits you. And I bet the girls enjoy the new bartender."

Jagger laughed and shrugged. "I've only enjoyed one conversation since I started." He winked at me and I rolled my eyes in return, trying to hide a grin. "All right, let me go find Dallas before he's got blood all over his face." With that, I turned to walk straight to the door that led to the cage downstairs. I knew where to find my brother since I knew about his routine before every fight. I walked to the changing room with his name written on the front in big, red letters. With a quick knock, I opened the door and saw Dallas punching and kicking a huge bag hanging from the ceiling. His coach Malakai, or just Kai, was standing on the other side of it, holding it in place so it was easier for Dallas to hit it. Kai was in his fifties and made a name for himself as an MMA fighter back when he was younger. Now, he had multiple body parts that didn't work properly, but it didn't stop him from training Dallas.

Dallas saw me enter the room and stopped moving, turning his head to look at me. "You're here." He sounded surprised.

"Imagine that," I mumbled, then glanced over at Malakai with a smile. "Hey, Kai. Haven't seen you in a while. How are you?" Not that his answer would've changed in the past few years. He was miserable. His body hurt every step he took, and I tried to explain to Dallas multiple times that if he kept on fighting, he would end up like Malakai. And at a young age, thirty maybe. And he was very close to that.

"I'm fine, sweetie. My wife was at your studio the other day. I love the painting she brought home." I smiled at that since I did have some customers here and there who bought my art.

"Glad you like it. Uh, Dal? Can I talk to you for a minute?" I turned my attention to Dallas, and he nodded, taking a sip from his water. Malakai took the hint and walked out of the room.

"What's up?" he asked, sitting down on the bench.

"So, Jagger got the job," I pointed out and he nodded. "Yeah, he's a fast learner, and the ladies like him."

Of course, that was one of the main reasons why Jagger got to work behind the bar. "I see. Can you do me a favor before he fully starts working here though? He got a call this morning from his sister. He has to go back to his hometown for three days to sign some papers. He asked me to go with him. I didn't want him to feel weird about asking you, especially after just getting the job."

Dallas eyed me for a while, and I could tell he was thinking about the *he asked me to go with him* part. He was being overprotective. I didn't like that. I was old enough to make my own decisions.

"Are you sure you wanna go with him? I mean, you don't know anyone there. What will you be doing all day when he's got his shit to handle?" Good question. But I didn't think that far, and I imagined Jagger wouldn't be signing papers all day long for three days straight.

"Let that be my concern," I told him.

"All right, sure. Just don't make me fire him when you're back and he's broken your heart." I rolled my eyes at him being overdramatic.

"Can you stop acting like a tough guy? I got this. Jagger's good to me. In the end, firing someone for that is a stupid reason. Just...let him take Tuesday through Thursday off and he'll be back at work on Friday." I was getting sick of his behavior. One day he likes Jagger, the next he acts like he's the enemy. It's not like I acted the way he did when he dated girls.

"Okay, okay. Calm down, Rusty. Now get out. I don't have a lot of time left here. The fight starts soon." I ignored the nickname I'd despised since I was little. It made me want to dye my hair many times in the past. But instead of letting Dallas destroy my mood, I thought about spending three full days with Jagger.

Chapter Seventeen

Jagger

I watched as Gray walked back upstairs with a slightly annoyed expression on her face. She obviously talked to her brother, since the way she looked was the same way Hunter looked when Bliss annoyed him. Harlow never got annoyed with me. At least, that's what I imagined.

I waited for Gray to come and talk to me about what Dallas said, and in the meantime, I mixed some cocktails for the two women sitting in front of me at the bar. This job wasn't too bad. People here were nice, if not a little too flirty. I even had a guy asking for my number, but I told him I wasn't allowed to flirt with customers or take their numbers. Not sure if that was a thing, but just some minutes ago, I couldn't stop flirting with Gray. *I'm dating her, so that's different*, I thought.

"Thank you, handsome. You're new in town,

right?" The fake blonde who ordered a Cosmopolitan let her eyes wander all over my upper body, then down my arms and back up to my face. Her hair ended right on her tits, which were impressively large. Probably went under the knife one too many times. Her icy blue eyes were distracting enough to keep mine off her breasts, thankfully.

"I am. Enjoy your drinks, ladies," I responded in the hopes that she wouldn't keep the conversation going. At first glance, she looked young. But taking a better look at her made me realize that this woman was at least ten years older than me.

"I'm Chelsea, and this is my friend Laine," she said with a smirk and I wished women would stop trying so hard when I obviously wasn't interested. I had my Gray I wanted to talk to. But being a bartender, flirting came with the territory. I had to get used to it. Also, not telling her my name could make her mad. I gave them a tight smile and nodded.

"Jagger. It's nice to meet you both." But that wasn't the end of this conversation either.

"So, tell me, Jagger…where are you from? And what made you come to Newton?" Chelsea was a real attention seeker, the way she pushed her elbows against the side of her breasts to make them seem even bigger. I kept my eyes on hers, trying not to fall for her little game.

"I'm from Nebraska. I needed a fresh start." I kept my sentences short because there was no fucking reason for her to know all about my past and reasons. I glanced over to the booth Gray was sitting at with Joey and Sage on the opposite. They were talking, and I could tell Gray wasn't in the mood for either of them.

"Fifteen minutes!" I heard Levi shout from the other side of the bar and people immediately started moving toward the door leading down to the cage. I looked over at him, then back at Gray. She wasn't watching the fight. The way she talked about Dallas's fights, I knew she wasn't going to follow Sage and her boyfriend downstairs. Again, I looked over at Levi, who was walking toward me. "You wanna go watch the fight?" he asked, taking a glance at Chelsea and her rather quiet and less annoying friend, Laine.

Neither of them was moving though, and I wondered if they wanted to see Dallas fight or not. "Uh, I think I'll stay up here." I didn't need a real reason to make Levi go. He just nodded and walked around the bar area to get to the door. Another look at Chelsea and Laine, and the less vocal one finally stood up from her stool. "Come on, Chelsea. Let's go see the fight. I bid on Dally."

I raised an eyebrow at Laine's nickname for Dallas. Did he know they called him Dally? "Yeah, you should go watch. He's great," I pushed, hoping Chelsea would finally get up off her ass and follow her friend.

"I don't know. I'd much rather sit here and talk to the new guy. Maybe some alone time will break the ice between us." I started to hate her voice. High pitched and annoying as fuck. She sounded like a child, which probably helped with older men, but my patience-meter was falling to the negatives.

"You should really go watch the fight," I urged, and my heart rate picked up as Gray came up behind Chelsea with a deep frown on her forehead.

"Ah, there you are, sweetheart." I smiled at Gray and hoped it didn't scare her off. I needed Chelsea to get off my back though. Calling Gray my sweetheart felt right in all kinds of ways and it made her smile bright. It appeared as if she wasn't sure what to say though.

Chelsea turned in her stool and looked at Gray, her expression hidden from me. Hopefully, she wasn't trying to scare her off. "Hello, Chelsea." Gray's voice didn't sound pleased. Shit, so they knew each other.

"Gray, so good to see you again. I didn't know you had a...boyfriend." Chelsea turned back to meet my eyes, then lifted her tattooed eyebrows and let out a laugh. "I'm sorry. I didn't think you liked girls like her." She got up from her stool, linked her arm with Laine's, and looked at Gray again. "I hope your brother wins tonight. I promised him a little surprise if he does."

They walked off, and all this time Chelsea was talking, I felt my insides heat up. That seemingly sweet act of hers was just a mask she put on to flirt. Her ugliness quickly showed the moment she realized another girl had my full attention over her.

The second the two friends were out of sight, Gray rolled her eyes and let out a growling noise. "What a bitch!" she exclaimed, then walked around the bar to stand by my side. I couldn't stop a chuckle escaping me, and I leaned against the counter, crossing my arms. "So, you know her?"

She laughed, throwing her head back, then closing her eyes and sighing. "Who *doesn't* know her? She's incredibly annoying. She's the senator's ex-wife. He filed for divorce some years ago because she was going out with college guys. I see she hasn't changed, the way she looked at you."

I puckered my lips, nodding quickly and then smiling at her. "If it makes you feel better, I was hoping for her to stop talking to me."

"I don't need you to make me feel better. I know her and I think I know you well enough. You wouldn't fall for her attempts of getting you naked and over her," Gray assured me, and I was glad she thought that way. Because it was true. I wasn't into older women anyway. Especially like Chelsea.

I smiled again, reaching for her waist, and pulling her against my body. My hands stayed on her lower back, with my thumb caressing her. I needed to change the subject. "What did Dallas say about our road trip?" I asked, looking down into her eyes.

They lit up the second I finished my sentence. "He's letting me go with you." Perfect.

A grin spread on my lips and I leaned down to kiss her cheek. "Can't wait. It will be fun."

Gray nodded, with her lips pressed together tightly and her eyes still sparkling. They moved to my lips, and her hands made their way over my chest, then stopped once her arms were wrapped around my neck. "Will you call me sweetheart again?"

Her voice was sweet and low, almost like a whisper. I grinned, loving the fact that she didn't miss that. "I was indecisive on whether or not to call you Rusty instead." That made her laugh, and one of her hands gripped the back of my head, pulling at my hair with just enough force.

"You're an idiot," she mumbled with a grin, then stood on her tiptoes to kiss my lips softly. Luckily, we were all alone at the bar since everyone else was watching the fight. I moved my hands over her bottom, squeezing it tightly to show her just how much I wished we were in my bedroom. Both of her hands were now buried inside my hair, tugging at it the way I liked her to.

I felt my heart speed up again, wishing her lips wouldn't feel so damn good against mine. Another part of my body started to move, and I felt my dick getting bigger in my pants. Our tongues touched, and I squeezed her ass once more before wrapping my arms around her back tightly.

"We should stop," she moaned against my lips, her words contradicting the sounds that came out of her mouth. But she was right. Someone could walk in on us any second, so I dipped my tongue into her mouth one last time before pulling back and getting some distance between us. I kept my eyes on hers, trying to figure out what she was thinking. She looked happy. Satisfied.

Something was still lingering on my mind and I needed an explanation for it. With a grin, I tilted my head and asked, "How many people call your brother Dally?"

Gray let out a laugh, throwing her head back again. *Fuck me*...I loved it when she did that. "Just Chelsea and Laine. I cringe every time I hear them say it."

CHAPTER EIGHTEEN

Gray

My gallery was open on Monday and I was working on a painting for an older guy who specifically asked for a portrait of his late wife. I wouldn't say I was bad at painting humans, but it wasn't my strong suit. I gave my all to resemble the beautiful young woman on the picture onto the canvas, to meet my customer's high expectations. The picture was of his wife in her early twenties, taken right after they got married in 1962. She looked happy, and her eyes did not hide the love she felt for her husband. Mr. Carlisle had told me things about her. What she loved, what she disliked, and all the ups and downs they had before and after marriage.

The painting of her was coming along slowly. I was careful not to overdo but capture all the small details her husband loved so much about her. The little mole right next to her left eye, or the dimple that only appeared on her left cheek when she smiled. Mr. Carlisle wanted me to capture just that. The little things.

I was concentrated on the neutral colors I was mixing on my palette so that I didn't notice the woman coming inside my gallery. I was in the studio in the back and watched as she walked around, eyeing the painting I was trying to sell. I put down my brush and palette, then walked toward the gallery to greet my guest.

"Hello, thank you for coming to my gallery. Is there something I can show you?" The woman turned to look at me, and with a tight smile, she nodded.

"Yes. I was looking for an abstract painting for my living room. I was thinking of some sort of...intense, violent art piece." Her voice was low, yet strong and determined. She was creeping me out, to be fully honest. And to request such a painting was also new to me. I looked over at my paintings and puckered my lips, trying to remember if I'd ever painted something "intense and violent." Not sure why anyone would want such a painting in their living room for everyone to see, but if that's what my new customer wanted, then I could give it to her.

"I don't think I've ever done such a painting, but I take requests." I smiled and grabbed the notebook from the table next to me and opened it on an empty page, ready to write in it. "I do any size of canvas, oil or acrylics, and the price will depend on the time it takes for me to finish it," I explained and looked back into her eyes. Something felt off, but I had many customers who didn't give me positive vibes but turned out to be the ones who paid a lot. I needed that to survive. To pay rent and eat every day.

"Sounds fair," the woman said and turned to look at one of the paintings again.

"Let's take a seat." I pointed to the two chairs in the corner of the gallery and she made her way toward them, sitting in the one next to the window. "One second," I told her, walking back to my studio and taking a bottle of water out of the mini fridge, then grabbing two glasses and walking back to where the woman was waiting on me. I put down the water and glasses, filled both up, and sat down on the empty chair. With my notebook open and ready on my lap, I looked up to start questioning her.

"May I have your name?" I asked, putting the end of my pen on the paper.

"Yes, Annie." That's all she said, and I didn't push to ask for her last name since she obviously wasn't going to tell me herself. I wrote down her name, then looked up again.

"And your phone number? So that I can contact you as soon as I'm done with the painting or if I have any questions during the process."

"I prefer email," she explained calmly, then went ahead and told me her email address.

The numbers in her email address resembled a birth date, but it was impossible for it to be hers since she was much older than someone born in 1993. Probably one of her children? Or maybe it was a special date for her. I wasn't digging deeper into that. Not my business.

"All right. So, intense and violent…" I wasn't sure how to start this conversation since my past paintings were never painted out of negativity, so I tried to start with the easier things.

"What colors do you have in mind?" I asked, giving Annie a smile, hoping to receive one in return instead of her deep frown.

"Dark blues and browns. Some black. Maybe with a hint of white here and there. White showing off the hope I feel. And the dark colors telling the story of my past. That horrible and hurtful time I had to live through with my own family."

Shit. That got dark very fast. I pressed my lips into a thin line, writing down what Annie was telling me. So, she had a troubled past including her family, but she still had hope. Well, that's good, right?

"And how would you envision the type of art matching your story? Realistic, or more abstract?" I was trying to figure out if there was more to the story, or if she would even let me in on it so I had more details.

"Abstract. It's a whirlwind. Nothing's clear, but there's something about it that lets everybody know there is still something to fight for, even if it looks dark and twisted." Her words made me shiver. Her eyes and the way she looked at me were empty, as if there was no emotion in them, yet her words contradicted them.

I wrote it down again, then bit my bottom lip and tried to imagine the canvas in front of me. "I have something in mind. What about the size of the canvas?" I pointed to a wall where there were five

110

different sized paintings, ranging from smallest to biggest.

She looked over at them, then quickly back to me. "The biggest one. This is a huge matter for me. And I want this painting to play a big part in my new home too." It didn't make much sense to me. Why would she want such a dark painting on her wall, when she's telling me right now how bad her past was? But then, I was just the artist. Whatever my customers want, I give them.

"That might take several weeks, but I will keep you updated, and you are always welcome to come by and look at it. If there's something you would like changed, it's best if you come by once a week or so," I told her. She nodded, then got up from her chair.

"Is there anything else?" she asked, already walking toward the exit. I quickly got up. "Yes, actually. There's a small deposit you have to pay right now just to assure you're taking this project seriously." I walked over to the counter where I had an already filled paper ready for customers to sign.

Annie looked up at me, then walked to the counter and stopped in front of it. I slid the paper over to her, pointing to a line where her signature would be going. "It's one hundred and fifty dollars for the big painting, and I accept cash and credit." I smiled again because she looked annoyed. I hated to make people give me money on the spot, but if they wanted a custom painting, they have to pay me first. Dallas made me start this policy since there were some teens months ago who messed with me and acted like they wanted a portrait painted of themselves. I started painting but never heard from them again. I wasted a shit load of paint and time. I don't want that to happen again.

Annie pulled out her wallet from her bag, zipped it open, and took out one hundred and fifty dollars cash out of it. She put the bills on the counter, then signed the paper, and looked back up at me. "I hope I won't be disappointed." With that, she turned and left my gallery, without any other word spoken.

I let out a breath. I was holding it in all the time she was here, and I didn't notice how nervous she made me feel. That woman was creepy. But now I had a big project to start working on and that I was excited about.

CHAPTER NINETEEN

Jagger

I told Gray to wait outside her apartment on Tuesday at eleven a.m. so we could get lunch before heading to Hastings without stopping on the way. I texted Low to let her know that we would be there in the afternoon, and she made sure to prepare my old bedroom for us to sleep in. I still had a spare key for the house, and we would stop there before heading to the diner to see my sister and Hunter. I was a little nervous to let Gray into my life and let her meet my family, but on the other hand, I was excited to spend some time with her.

My car stopped in front of Gray, who was standing there, waiting with a small duffle bag next to her feet. I got out of the car and walked over to her, smiling back while she lifted the bag from the ground.

"Nice car," she told me, then grabbed my

113

sweatshirt with one hand and leaned in to kiss me softly. I put both my hands on either side of her head, kissing her back and holding her close for a few seconds and enjoying her lips on mine. I loved how comfortable we were with each other, even openly on the street, yet I had to find out where this was heading. We felt good when we spent time together, and we acted as if we were a couple. Well, we were dating, but dating itself had such a huge range between *we're just figuring things out but let's have fun for now* and *I really like this person and hope I could call him or her my boyfriend or girlfriend*. Personally, I was leaning toward the second one, but I had to find out where Gray was standing.

I leaned back, licking my lips, and looking into her eyes with a smug grin. "Glad you like it. You ready?" I grabbed the bag from her hand and opened the trunk to put it inside, next to my duffle bag. I made sure not to pack too much, and Gray's bag wasn't heavy either.

"Where do you park your car? I've never seen it when I came over to your place." I closed the trunk and turned back to her, then looked at the car I considered the only non-human thing I loved.

"Around the block. A little hidden and secure. I don't want anyone to hit it while parking in that narrow parking space in front of the building," I explained, hoping that it didn't sound weird.

Gray nodded, eyeing the car again with a smile. "Isn't a car like this expensive as hell?"

I shrugged, pushing my fists into my front pockets. "I restored it when I was working at the mechanic's. I saw it at a scrapyard while looking for some pieces for the other cars, so I bought it and worked on it whenever I got the time to. It's a Mustang Coupe from the year 1967. Old on the outside, but pretty new on the inside." I loved my car a little too much. Not sure if Gray was really interested in it, or just trying to make conversation.

No, she seems fairly interested. We never talked about anything either of us was annoyed with, I thought. I was not going to be unsure about this now. If she wasn't interested, she wouldn't have agreed to come to Hastings with me. She wants to be here.

"I like it," she assured me, then nodded toward the car. "Should we go?"

"Yes, here." I opened the door to the passenger seat and let her get inside. Closing the door again, I walked around the car and got in myself, immediately putting on the seatbelt. Gray did the same, then leaned back and sighed. "I'm so excited to see your old hometown. I'll admit…I went on Google Earth to check it out."

I chuckled, then started the car. "And what did you think of it? A little broken-down small town, huh?" I said with a grin because Hastings wasn't as appealing as Newton for people to visit.

"I think it looks interesting. And I bet it's better than on Google Earth. I can't wait to meet your sister and Hunter." I could hear her smile in her voice, so I kept my eyes on the street in front of me. "Harlow's excited too. You'll like each other," I assured her and put my right hand on her thigh to give it a squeeze.

"So, we'll be staying in your old home?" Gray asked and I nodded. "Low wants to use my room for the nursery, but my things are still in there. I gotta warn you already. The walls are quite thin in that house." That was enough of a hint for her since she let out a small laugh and shrugged. "I think I can handle that. They're a couple. It's normal, and I've often heard Dallas when we still lived at our parents' home."

Well, that was awkward. I heard Harlow and Hunter once or twice, and I wasn't that easygoing when it happened the first time. Punching Hunter was necessary at that time, but that was also because it was the first time I found out that he'd slept with my baby sister.

"All right...let's change the subject," I laughed, then looked at the dashboard, showing the time. "Is it too early for you to get some lunch already?"

"I could go for some food right now, sure," Gray answered, then placed her hand on mine, which was still on her thigh. She squeezed my fingers, then started caressing the back of my hand softly.

I enjoyed it, hoping when we'd get back in the car she would continue doing it. I turned into the first diner I saw, parked, and turned to look at her. "Let's get some food then." With a smile, she nodded and got out of the car, and I did the same, taking her hand as she stepped next to me. I linked my fingers with hers, then lifted her hand to my mouth to kiss it. "You make me feel good."

I wasn't sure why that came out of me so unexpected, but I'm somehow glad it did. My words made Gray smile brighter than ever, and she leaned into me while we walked toward the entrance of the diner. "I feel the same, Jagger."

Chapter Twenty

Gray

We sat down at an empty booth and immediately looked at the menu. I didn't eat breakfast, and a burger sounded good. I looked up at Jagger, who was studying the card still, with a little crease between his eyes.

"Want some recommendations?" I offered, then pointed to the burger section. "I really like their beef burgers here. With some extra cheese. And maybe a side of fries."

Jagger kept studying the menu and then nodded after a while. "Sounds good," he exclaimed, putting the menu back down and looking at me with a smile. "Do you come here often? It's not far from town."

I nodded, then looked around the diner and smiled back at him at the memories that flashed through my mind. "Our parents took us here at least once a month. And we spent most of our birthdays here. It's also where I had my first job when I started high school. I got to help in the kitchen washing the dishes, then I helped waiting tables when I was eighteen. They even let me help make pancakes in the morning." I was proud of that time and my grin showed it. "The people here changed, though. I barely know anyone, but the cooks are equally as great as the old ones."

"Well, I can't wait to try the burger. I love when people are amazed by the littlest things, and you certainly are one of them." His smile never faded while I told him the story of my first job, and the way he was genuinely interested in me and my past felt good.

I smiled back, then turned to look for a waitress to hide my cheeks turning pink. The tingles in my stomach appeared again, just like that night at The Red, and that time I spent with him in his apartment. I tried to slow down my feelings from growing too fast but pushing them aside was not possible.

"What can I get for you today?" The waitress was a young, blonde girl, probably in high school. She seemed sweet, her smile letting us know that she liked this job just as much as I liked it when I worked here.

I smiled back at her, then glanced at the menu to remember what we wanted to eat. "We'll both have the beef burger with extra cheese. And I'll have lemonade to drink."

The girl nodded and wrote down my order, then turned to look at Jagger without her smile ever fading. "And for you?" she asked, ready to write down his drink. Jagger quickly studied the menu, his lips puckering while he was thinking.

"I'll have an iced tea," he said, then looked back at me. "Let's see if it tastes just as good as Harlow's." A grin spread on his lips, and I remembered him telling me the story about his sister's famous iced tea which she made since she was little.

"Our iced tea is delicious. I drink it every time I get the chance." The fascination in the girl's voice was adorable. I looked at her name tag, revealing that she was called Maya. I looked back up, remembering the time I drank all the iced tea they made here.

"Do you guys also get to eat all the leftovers that didn't make the plates? I worked here too a few years ago," I told her. She grinned and nodded, looking at both of us with wide eyes. "The cook sometimes does it on purpose so we can have dinner all together after the diner's closed."

"Sounds like a nice place to work," Jagger said, then leaned back and kept his smile up. I agreed, just like Maya, then she left toward the kitchen.

"Sweet kid," Jagger said, and I nodded with a sigh.

"I remember wearing that uniform. It fit me like a glove, and I looked good in it. We always got compliments when we were working and that sure boosted my confidence." I laughed.

"I saw you wear a skirt last weekend. I can only imagine how hot you'd look in a uniform like that." He grinned, then looked around the diner before his eyes landed on mine again. His expression was slightly more serious now, and I wondered what it was that changed his mood.

I tilted my head. "What's wrong?" I asked, hoping it was nothing too serious.

"I talked to Harlow this morning and she told me that Bliss found out that we're visiting Hastings for a few days." He stopped, eyeing me carefully. I remembered Bliss. The girl he had sex with but never had a relationship with or even dated. I slowly nodded, letting him know to continue.

"I've told you that Bliss and I have had some history, but it's over now. I know how she can act when something bothers her, and I don't want to scare you off, but I can't keep her from coming around either. She's family. Hunter's sister and Harlow's friend."

His voice was calm, but I could tell he was unsettled with the whole situation. Before I answered, Maya arrived with our drinks, and we thanked her before she went on to serve other guests.

"I'm excited to meet your family, Jagger. We can't change the past, so I guess we'll just see how it goes and adjust while it's happening." I smiled again, reaching for his hand, and squeezing it. "I might even get along with Bliss. I don't think she's a bad person. As long as she doesn't see me as the enemy, I think I'll be fine."

He slowly nodded, studying my face carefully. "Okay," he started, then looked down at his iced tea.

"Try it. Let's see if Harlow's is better." Changing the subject was the best thing to do. I couldn't stop Bliss from being a part of his life, but

I did feel a little lost, knowing that I would be the odd one out. I also had no idea what to expect from Harlow and Hunter. Jagger has always said that they're both nice people, but they haven't met me yet, and the possibility that they won't like me was still huge.

I watched Jagger take a sip from the iced tea, and his eyes immediately told me that he liked it. "Good, huh?" I grinned.

He nodded, taking another sip, then put his glass down again. "It tastes great. But I can't push Harlow's to second place. After all, she probably would kill me if she found out that I like someone's iced tea better than hers."

I laughed, nodding at his theory. "I won't tell," I promised, and our smiles grew as we kept looking at each other.

CHAPTER TWENTY-ONE

Jagger

Our food came quickly, but we took our time eating. The burger was as good as Gray said it would be and I enjoyed it with the iced tea I ordered.

"How was work yesterday?" Gray asked, taking a bite of her burger.

"There wasn't much going on. Dallas came by and we mostly just talked. Have you seen him since the fight? He's got some pretty bad bruises on his face."

She shook her head, sighing at my words and rolling her eyes. "I hate seeing him like that. He's broken his nose one too many times and his black eyes were an accessory he wore often. Did he at least win that fight?"

"Yeah, he did. The other guy had to get stitched up right after. I've fought against lots of crazy guys, but I would never get in that cage with your brother. He's a beast," I said sincerely. Dallas was insane.

123

He showed me a video of the fight someone took and put on the internet, and the way Dallas launched at his opponent was scary as hell. Even for me. At one point, you could even see the other guys' nose crack open from one simple punch. It reminded me of that one time I broke my nose at a fight. It wasn't pretty and lying to Low was even more painful than the fight itself.

"I just wish he would stop. He's got a business he earns enough money with. He just can't stop with the punching and hurting others. He needs someone to pull him down to earth. And those older women don't help. I've set him up on some dates before, but he would just screw them over and invite them to his next fight. I wish there was one girl who would finally show him that there's more than just the underground to be proud of."

It was funny that the second she told me how much she'd love for Dallas to have a girl on his side who would talk back instead of being pushed away, Bliss came to mind. But I kept that thought to myself. Although, she was the kind of girl to do whatever the fuck she wanted instead of being played by a guy like Dallas. It was different with me and her. She wanted me to test if she was ready to settle down. She talked about feelings a lot, even though we both knew it was all bullshit. Bliss tried hard to be loved, but I was the wrong guy for her. We both knew it.

"He'll get over it sooner or later. I did too," I assured her, because the thought of one day not being able to walk again was scary. I've seen Malakai, his coach. And he looked weak. It's not that Dallas didn't see the danger in fighting, it's that he didn't *want* to see it.

"What about you? How are the paintings coming along?" I asked to change the subject. Gray smiled at first, but it faded fast when a thought rushed through her mind. "There's this woman who came by and requested the weirdest painting ever," she said with her nose scrunched. "She wants this dark, twisted painting. Intense and violent, she said. With dark colors, but with a small hint of white, to accent the hope she still has. I've never done such a painting."

I studied her face for a while, wondering why someone would request such a painting. It was weird, to be honest. But then, there are lots of crazy people on this planet. I've known one all my life. But now that he's gone, I don't feel that storm inside of me anymore. Since Dean's death, I only had to get rid of the guilt still swirling around in my head, but that was starting to settle down slowly. Gray took my mind off it, and I was glad she did.

"I'm sure you'll nail that painting. You're talented as hell, and when you're done with hers, I'm going to request one too." With a grin, I took another sip of my drink, then reached over to take her hand on the table. "I'd like to watch you paint one day if that doesn't bother you too much."

Her eyes widened, and her cheeks turned pink once again. "I'm not sure I could concentrate with a handsome guy like you staring at me while I work." Her voice was soft and honest, with a hint of shyness. Fuck me, she got sweeter each damn time.

"Believe me, love. I most times can't concentrate

even by having you close." *There we go*, I thought, *it's happening too fucking fast.* I needed to slow down if I wanted us to work. But she made it hard for me. I liked her. A lot. Though, the way she looked at me told me that she was all in too. Why slow down?

Gray kept looking at me, her hand still in mine, warm and soft. My eyes fell to her lips, wishing I could pull her over here and kiss them. But my thoughts of kissing her the way we've done before were pushed aside as Maya stopped at our booth, looking down at our plates.

"Did you enjoy the burgers?" she asked, ready to take the plates back to the kitchen.

I snapped out of my imagination and looked up at her with a nod. "They were great, thank you," I told her, and Gray agreed with my words by nodding.

"Yes, delicious as always," she added, then let go of my hand to sit up straight again. The color on her cheeks didn't fade, and I couldn't help a chuckle. Maya took our empty plates and asked if we would like another drink.

"No, thank you. We should be going," I explained. "I'd like to pay," I added, and Maya nodded, walking back to the kitchen. I took another glance at Gray, her bottom lip caught between her teeth. "You okay?" I grinned, knowing I made her blush with my words.

"I'll have to get used to your flirting," was all she said. I shrugged, letting her know that she was right. I couldn't help myself with her. She made me want to flirt and compliment her. I wanted her to

126

know that I was all in for her. Only her. But without pushing too far and scaring her off.

After I paid for our meals, we said goodbye to Maya and headed out to my car. Before I pulled out my keys, I looked around the parking lot to make sure we weren't observed. No one was around, and with the other cars parked around us, I took the chance to push Gray against the passenger door, cupping her face in mine and pressing my lips to hers, making her squeal and then moan. Her hands immediately grabbed onto my sweater, pulling me closer and leaning back onto the car. Our lips moved against each other, and the tip of our tongues touched each time our lips parted. I wished I could take her back home and get into bed with her, making out like last Saturday. That had to wait, though.

My right hand moved from her cheek to her waist, holding her tight and then moving further down to the side of her ass. Since she was pushed against the car, and I had no way to move my hand between her and the door. I pulled her forward so my hand cupped her bottom. Another moan escaped her, and I knew she enjoyed the way I grabbed her while we were kissing. Touching her felt good, and I wondered what it would be like sleeping with her. I wanted to know what she desired. I'd have to find out someday, but for now, teasing her was exciting.

As the kiss deepened, I heard a car door slam, then a motor being turned on. I wasn't ready to let go yet, but as the car was backing up and moving closer, my lips left Gray's and I looked over to the car driving away. The second I looked inside it, I couldn't quite make out the driver, but the woman in it looked familiar. She was elderly, but it didn't occur to me who it was.

"Everything okay?" Gray asked, out of breath, and I moved my hand back up to her waist. I watched the car drive onto the main road, then turned to look at her.

"Yeah, I thought I knew that woman from somewhere. I've probably seen her around town sometime." I smiled at her now, forgetting about the woman who looked so familiar. I leaned into her again, kissing her one more time, then nodding down to my car. "Let's go. We have a long drive ahead of us."

CHAPTER TWENTY-TWO

Gray

The drive to Hastings was fun. We were listening to the radio, and with each song that came on, we told each other what we thought about it and why we liked or disliked it. Turned out that we had similar tastes. As "I'm On Fire" from Bruce Springsteen came on, Jagger's smile grew, and by looking at his facial expression, I could tell he liked the singer a lot. And hearing the song while I was keeping my eyes on him touched something inside me. Jagger always seemed old-school to me. In a good way, of course. He's a gentleman, he had a way with words, and he never acted up to make me feel uncomfortable when I was around him when we were alone or in public.

That's one major thing I needed to be comfortable with. A man who knows how to act in certain situations, keeping his cool and reacting to things normally without making a fool out of himself. Joey is one of those guys I would never date. Not sure how Sage does it, but I would be uneasy if the guy I was dating ever acted like Joey in front of others. He was loud and always had to say something, even if the conversation was not directed toward him.

Jagger was calm. He probably counted to thirty before he said something, just to make sure he wasn't saying anything to offend anyone or make him seem rude for interrupting others. He was respectful, and I was happy that he had chosen me to date and take with him to his hometown.

"This song is nice too," I heard Jagger say, and I blinked, noticing that a new song had started playing. I listened, then frowned because I couldn't name the singer. "Sounds like Oasis," I said with a look in his direction. His eyes were fixated on the road, with his left hand holding the steering wheel and the other covering mine again.

"Very close. They split up in 2009," he explained, and I nodded since I remembered the feud between the Gallagher Brothers. "So…this is an old song?" I asked. I didn't really keep up with famous people, but I was always up to learn about them when someone had something nice to say about them. All I listened to were Spotify playlists I put together or looked for on the app to get in the mood to paint. But I never searched up for a specific artist to listen to.

"Sounds like it, right?" Jagger said with a smile, then shook his head. "It's Liam Gallagher. I guess his style of making music remained the same throughout the years, even without the band. It's a great song." He nodded toward the radio, then glanced at me before turning his attention on the road again. I smiled back at him, then listened to the lyrics. At the chorus, I could hear Jagger sing along in a soft voice.

The way he sang the words sparked something in him, as if he were the one who wrote the song, meaning each word.

"This song has a strong meaning for you," I whispered, a smile still on my lips. He shrugged, then licked his bottom lip. "There's a reason why I left Hastings. It felt wrong staying there after..." Jagger stopped himself, and his face showed an expression I hadn't seen before. His eyes seemed to tear up, but the way his jaw tensed let me know he was fighting whatever emotion wanted to come out. I turned in my seat, lacing my fingers through his and putting my right hand on top of his.

"You don't have to talk about it if you don't want to," I assured him, even though I would've loved to get to know him better. Maybe I could help him get over whatever was bothering him.

He shook his head. "Now isn't the time to talk about it," he told me, then squeezed my hand and smiled at me quickly. "We're almost there. Fifteen minutes." I nodded and patted his hand, hoping whatever it was that bothered him had a way to disappear soon, with or without my help.

***

Jagger's old home was not what I expected. I imagined him growing up in a nice family home with his parents and sister, maybe a big backyard and a garage where he would work on old cars and repair them just like he did with his car. But the thought of a simple bungalow never entered my mind. I wasn't judging. It's a nice home, and I wasn't going to judge him for it. Also, he never talked about his parents living here too. He only said that Harlow and Hunter lived here now, so their parents might've moved out.

Jagger grabbed our bags out of the trunk, and I closed it afterward. "This is it," he mumbled, sounding nervous.

"It's cute. So, your sister's not home, right?"

Jagger shook his head. "We'll settle in and then go to the diner this evening. They both work late tonight, but Low said we'll have dinner together."

"Sounds good. I can't wait to meet them," I said with a smile, then followed him up the path to the front door. After he unlocked the door, he stepped aside to let me in. I walked past him, and immediately was greeted by the smell of wood and cinnamon. I took in a deep breath, wondering how a home could ever smell this good.

"Jesus Christ." Jagger chuckled, closing the door behind me. "Hunter didn't lie when he said that it constantly smelled like Christmas in here. Harlow is into candles now. I guess she lights them as soon as she comes into the house."

I looked around and surely found the first set of candles on a small table, sitting between two doors. "It smells amazing, to be honest," I admitted, turning back around to look at Jagger. "Show me around." I smiled, holding out my hand for him to take. He put down the bags, then slid his fingers through mine and nodded toward the living room. "We spent most of our time in here, Hunter and me. The kitchen's not really in use since they mostly eat at the diner." He pointed toward the kitchen on the other end of the living room.

I nodded, taking it all in. There was a big couch and a recliner, which looked old but comfy. Then there was a record player in one corner, with a big shelf holding vinyl records. The style of the furniture was vintage, and I imagined Jagger still living here. Well, the apartment he lived in now was also very nicely furnished, with a few things missing. But we talked about that already, and we'll probably look for the missing pieces sooner or later.

Jagger pulled me toward the two rooms on the other side of the hallway. He opened the one nearest to the front door. "This is, well, was my room. We'll stay in here." I looked inside, eyeing the bed like the one he had in his apartment and a small dresser, which didn't seem to fit a lot of clothes. There was nothing else in there, but I liked how minimal it was. In the end, he didn't come here often anymore.

The other room was Harlow and Hunter's bedroom. It looked like they bought some new things, but all in all, the room wasn't very special. A little bit like mine, simple but cozy.

"And that's the bathroom. They renovated it, the kitchen will be next, I think."

"It's a nice home, but…" I looked around, noticing there were no more rooms in the house. "Where did your parents sleep? Did you share a room with Harlow before they moved out?"

Jagger stopped, then looked at me with what looked like shame flashing in his eyes. I was quick to comfort him. "It's not weird to share a bedroom with your sister. I had sleepovers with Dallas all the time when we were little," I told him, but his expression didn't change. Shit, did I say something wrong?

"I'm sorry...I didn't mean to—"

"Don't apologize. It's a fair question," he assured me, then pulled me back to the living room to sit on the couch. He turned to me, looking at our hands on his lap. I didn't understand what he meant because I was sure I had upset him.

"It's a bit difficult, you know." His voice wasn't as confident as before, and his eyes stayed on our hands, not looking up into mine. I felt bad because I had put him in this situation. I didn't mean to push him to talk, but I wasn't stopping him now. I said enough already.

"Harlow and I moved in here when I was old enough to get a house. She was still young, and we had some issues with our parents. Well, with our dad, to be specific." He stopped, and his eyes were on mine now.

"Our parents aren't around anymore, but we're good now. I mean, Harlow's happy and I moved to Newton. There's nothing to worry about, I just didn't think I would get so fucking emotional coming back here. Just know that nothing's wrong, all right?" He smiled, lifting his hand to cup my cheek. "I'm glad we're here and I'm excited for you to meet my family."

I let his words linger in my mind for a while,

before deciding that I wasn't going to judge him for his past. Why would I? I had no right to and I liked the man he was today. "I can't wait to meet them." I smiled back, leaning in to kiss his lips. His lips moved against mine, and he pulled me closer. I could feel him grinning into the kiss, and I pushed my fingers into his hair to tug on it. There was a reason why Jagger wasn't as wild as other men his age. His behavior was relaxed and attentive, making sure everyone around him felt safe and happy. And that's how I wanted it to be. No negativity and no past events changed the way I felt about this man.

Chapter Twenty-Three

Jagger

As we pulled onto Frankie's Diner's parking lot, I let my eyes wander over the diner I spent so much time at. It didn't change much after Hunter and Harlow renovated it, but it was strange since I'd only seen it with a crumbling façade and dirty windows. The sign stayed the same, but each letter was lit, not like before when half of them needed new LED lights inside of them. It looked better, and by the pictures Low sent me, I knew the inside was still the way Frankie left it. Only cleaner.

I turned to look at Gray, who was pulling the hood of her jacket over her head. "You weren't kidding about the rain." She grinned.

I nodded, looking out the window and up to the sky. "It comes and goes, but I think it'll stop before we leave later tonight." I knew Hastings' weather too well.

"Are you ready?" I asked with a smile and opened the car door. Gray nodded once, then stepped out. I did the same, locking the car and pushing the keys into the pocket of my jacket. "All right, here goes nothing," I murmured, hoping them meeting for the first time went well. With Gray next to me, we walked to the entrance of the diner and I held open the door for her, then I followed. I was surprised by the people sitting in the many booths. Last year, you would only see older men sitting here, maybe eating something or just reading the newspaper. But now it was the opposite. Young people, teenagers, and college students filled the booths, eating full meals. Their laughter filled the whole diner, and the music playing in the background was soothing, making this place feel at home. Harlow insisted on buying a jukebox to play vinyls and for her to switch them out whenever she wanted to change the vibe of the music.

Gray's fingers touched mine softly, and I looked at her with a smile. "Nice, huh? It's great to be back," I told her. I tried to push that one thought of what happened last year aside, not wanting to remember what went down with my father. It was incredible how Harlow wanted to work in here and keep Frankie's legacy up, but then, she was strong enough to forget about the bad and horrible things that happened in her past. That's why people adored her. And that's why she was able to forgive Hunter for his past.

Before Gray could answer, I heard my name being called out from afar. "You're finally here!" My sister appeared from behind the counter, and she was quick to reach me and throw her arms around my neck. I chuckled, hugging her tight and kissing the side of her head while she kept her arms locked around me.

"I missed you, sweet girl," I whispered, watching Hunter come our way with a smug grin. His eyes shifted to Gray, who was still standing beside me, if not a few steps behind me to not bother our sibling reunion.

"I'm so happy you're here. I missed you." I could tell she was happy, but there was a slight hint of sadness to her voice. I wasn't leaving for another two days, but she was already upset that I would leave. I wished I could stay, but Hastings wasn't my home anymore. Not for now.

When she pulled back, she stepped away to let Hunter reach me, and without hesitation, I hugged him and patted his back. "Good to see you, man," I told him, and he nodded, not letting our hug last for more than five seconds before stepping back again to stand next to my sister.

Hunter's eyes were on Gray again, and I reached back, grabbing her hand, and pulling her to my side. Now that she was here, I wasn't sure what to say. Hunter didn't show many emotions most of the time, but I could tell he was trying to figure out if he accepted Gray or not. Harlow, on the other hand, was beaming.

"This is Gray Washington. I told you guys about her before," I explained, but they knew already. I told them about her before we had our second date, but I had to be polite and introduce her. Harlow stepped forward, hugging Gray tightly, then moving.

"It's so nice to meet you, Gray. I'm Harlow.

Jagger wasn't kidding when he said that you're beautiful." Of course, now was the time for my sister to put me on the spot and let Gray know that I've talked to my sister about her already. Gray's smile grew and she glanced at me for a second, amusement dancing in her eyes. When her eyes left mine, she continued the conversation with Harlow.

"It's nice to meet you too. Jagger's told me a lot about you." Her voice was calm, and I could tell they were already comfortable with each other. Hunter, on the other hand, hadn't said a word yet. When I raised an eyebrow, he imitated my facial expression and Harlow nudged his side to make him talk. Not sure why he acted this way now, but I had a feeling it had to do with Bliss. He knew what happened between his sister and me, and he was trying to figure out if I had the same intentions with Gray.

He snapped out of his thoughts, then turned to look at Gray with a tight smile. "Hunter. Nice to meet you, Gray," he said in a low voice, not showing much emotion.

"You too," Gray replied with a smile, and I prayed to God that they were going to get along. I wasn't saying that they didn't like each other, but Hunter was an asshole most of the time, and I needed him to relax and let me handle my dating life on my own.

"All right, big guy." Harlow laughed, patting Hunter's chest. "Go back to the kitchen to prepare our food. I bet these two are starving after that long drive."

Hunter didn't hesitate to do what she told him,

and I forgot how pussy-whipped he was when it came to Harlow. It was entertaining to watch, considering he wouldn't take shit from anyone. Not even me at times. So, he nodded, then got back to the kitchen, leaving us three standing there by the door.

"He'll take a break to eat with us but let's sit down already. It won't take long." Harlow turned around and walked toward an empty booth with a *reserved* sign on the table. I smiled at Gray and nodded toward my sister. As we reached her, I let Gray slide over to the window, and I sat down next to her. My hand squeezed her thigh, and hers covered mine to assure me that she was all right and felt comfortable.

Harlow stopped a waitress who was passing by with a filled tray, then asked us what we wanted to drink.

"I'd like to try that iced tea Jagger always talks about," Gray said to Harlow and received a wide smile from her.

"Two pitchers of our iced tea. Thank you, Aggie." Low sat down on the other side of the booth.

"My head is all over the place lately, and I'm glad I have Hunter to think about all the things I forget so easily. My body is playing tricks with me too. One day I feel like eating five steaks at once, the next I can't even hold in water."

Gray smiled, tilting her head to the side. "Congratulations on the pregnancy. Jagger told me," she said, sounding almost apologetic. Harlow's face lit up, and I knew they would be talking about this for a while before I was able to say something. Besides, I'd heard it all already. The many phone calls I had with Harlow were sweet, but I knew Gray would handle some topics better than me. So, I let them talk and get to know each other. I kept caressing Gray's leg, making her feel welcome and wanted.

"We're so excited to meet him. Or her." Harlow's brows furrowed. "We don't know the gender yet…but I have this strange feeling that it's a boy." Now, a smile appeared on her lips and Gray was all ears. "Hunter thinks it's a girl, but I can't imagine him with a little girl around the house. But then, I think it would be funny to see him handle a teenage girl someday," Harlow laughed, and I grinned at the thought of that.

"Oh, God, let it be a girl," I prayed.

"Anyway, enough of my pregnancy. How did you two meet?"

Gray didn't mind answering that question or talking about us to my sister. I knew it wouldn't be a problem to get them to like each other, but I was hoping Hunter wouldn't keep his strange mood up with Gray. Even if she handled him well just then, I hoped he'd accept who I was dating. In the end, it was none of his business, anyway.

"He moved into an apartment block where my brother and my cousin Sage live. She invited us both to a party and that's where I first saw him." Gray looked over at me with a soft smile, and I squeezed her thigh once again. "I wasn't sure about him at first, but after getting to know him a little better, I knew I had to give him a chance."

Harlow had a huge grin on her face now, and I chuckled. She probably knew what Bliss and I had was over, since they were close and talked a lot. I was glad Harlow liked Gray so much. "Well, I think he's the greatest guy on earth. And you both look happy, so you're both doing something right here."

Harlow always knew what to say to let others feel special. And the way she looked at Gray told me I made the right decision asking her out. As long as Harlow had a smile on her face, I had no reason to feel as if I was doing the wrong thing.

Gray turned to look at me, a soft smile appearing on her lips. "Yeah, I think he's great too."

CHAPTER TWENTY-FOUR

Gray

Hunter was a great cook. I'd give him that. But he hadn't warmed up to me yet and the looks he gave Jagger told me that he wasn't yet over what Jagger had with Bliss. I knew about Hunter and Bliss being siblings, but Jagger never said a thing about them caring about who they dated. Maybe Hunter just wanted his sister to be with Jagger, but that wasn't the case and I hoped he would understand sooner or later. In the end, if what Jagger and I had was going to last, he somehow had to adjust to us being a couple.

"Did you enjoy the steak? It's one of Hunter's specialties. He can cook anything, Harlow said, her eyes full of admiration for her boyfriend and soon to be the father of her first child. You could feel their love in the whole diner, and the way they communicated with each other without even speaking was adorable. As if they could read each other's minds.

143

"It was delicious, thank you," I replied with a smile. I made eye-contact with Hunter again, and he was studying me closely. He didn't know what to think of me, and his stare made me uncomfortable. He was protective over Harlow, but also Jagger. And to be fair, Hunter was a big, intimidating guy. He was well built, and his face was hard to read.

"All right, man. Give her a break." Jagger chuckled, then cupped the back of my head with his fingers buried into my hair. "Gray's an amazing woman, and I would appreciate it if you'd stop looking at her as if she's done something wrong. Is this about Bliss?" Jagger asked. I was surprised how openly they talked about things, especially if a certain someone was Hunter's sister and Jagger's ex in one. I scrunched up my nose, hoping this conversation wouldn't be awkward.

"Nah, that's not it." Hunter's voice had a hint of amusement in it, that much I heard. His eyes moved to Jagger, and I braced myself for what he would say next. If he's not mad about Jagger not seeing his sister anymore, or the fact that he ended things with her, why was he so damn mysterious? I wondered if Harlow had to keep up with him behaving like this. But then, she seemed to have him under control.

"I was glad to hear you two weren't fucking around anymore. You guys were toxic as hell. I'm just trying to figure her out," Hunter said, his eyes back on mine again. Now, the amusement I heard in his voice before also appeared in his eyes, and the corner of his mouth turned up into a smug grin.

"Well, don't." Jagger sounded annoyed with his best friend.

"I think she's great, Hunter," Harlow announced, then smiled at me brightly. "I know when Jagger's happy, and he certainly is with Gray by his side. And talking about his past lovers won't help. Jag's happy. It's been a while, and I wanna keep it that way."

The three of them shared something right then. A memory. Something they lived through and hoped to forget again as soon as possible. All their faces fell for a second, but the pain that flashed through their eyes quickly vanished again. They didn't want to show any sign of weakness.

I glanced at my hands, not sure about what to say. There obviously was something in their past that scarred them deeply, and Harlow talking that way about him made it clear that Jagger was broken before.

"Thanks, sweet girl," Jagger said to her, then reached over to my hands, sliding his fingers through mine. I turned to look at him, and I mimicked his smile, letting him know I was okay.

"I didn't mean to offend or scare you in any way, Gray," Hunter told me. "Just making sure my brother here made the right choice dating you."

I nodded and smiled, then looked back at Jagger, unsure of what to say. I usually talked a lot, but Hunter still made me nervous. As long as Jagger was happy, I was too. But I still found it weird how they just pushed Bliss to the side. If a guy treated Sage the way Jagger treated Bliss, I would go apeshit on him just to teach him a lesson. But then, I didn't know the whole story. And I didn't know Bliss. It wasn't my business. If Jagger wanted to talk about his past with Bliss, I would hear him out. Otherwise, I wasn't going to dig.

"Stop thinking too much," Jagger whispered, leaning in, and kissing my temple. "You're here with me, and I wouldn't want any other girl by my side." His words always had a way of making me feel special. I smiled, knowing my cheeks were turning pink.

"Right, we'll let you two talk. I gotta go back to work." Hunter stood up and helped Harlow out of the booth. "Low and I will stay at the trailer while you're here. We don't wanna wake you guys when we get up early to go to work." With that, Hunter headed back to the kitchen, leaving Harlow standing in front of our booth. "I'll finish some paperwork. Come say bye before you leave, okay?" She leaned down to kiss Jagger's cheek, and with one more smile, she followed Hunter.

Jagger let out a deep breath. "Sorry about that," he apologized, looking back into my eyes. "Especially Hunter. He doesn't really think before he speaks or acts. Had to get used to that years ago."

I shook my head to let him know that I wasn't offended or hurt. "He wants the best for you. Just like Harlow. I liked them. I guess we'll just have to get to know each other a little better before we know how to act with one another. But I'm glad I came, really."

He studied my face for a while, before nodding and kissing the corner of my mouth softly. "I just feel like I owe you something. An explanation about…Bliss."

I wasn't going to stop him since an explanation sounded so much better than just wondering what happened. I mean, before we started dating, I knew there were no feelings involved in whatever they had, but his full side of the story might clear some thoughts I had about their past.

"Of course, I'll listen," I whispered.

With a nod, he pulled me closer to his side and kissed my head. "Tonight."

CHAPTER TWENTY-FIVE

Jagger

After saying goodbye to Harlow and Hunter, we left the diner and drove back home. It was sweet of them to spend the next few nights at Hunter's old trailer, and they didn't seem to mind at all. I'd been to Hunter's trailer a lot when we still worked together. He kept it clean, and the neighbors weren't as bad as people would think. Harlow was safe, and that's what was important to me.

"I can't wait to try this cake," Gray announced as we stepped into the house. I chuckled, locking the door behind me and nodding. "It's a great cake. Make yourself at home. I'll get us another plate and something to drink." I took the cake slices Gray was holding from her hands and walked to the kitchen.

Instead of her getting comfortable on the couch, Gray came up next to me and opened the cabinet above her head. Lucky for her, the plates were hiding in there and she grabbed one, then closed the cabinet again. "I think I would drive all the way from Newton just to eat at the diner," she said, then lifted one of the slices over to the empty plate. "Honestly, I've not eaten this good since I last went to visit my parents on Christmas, and that's almost three months ago."

I puckered my lips and turned to look into her eyes with a raised brow. "Are you saying the burgers we ate last week weren't tasty?" I challenged, obviously joking.

Gray laughed, then shook her head. "Your burgers were incredible. But let's be honest...you used Hunter's recipe, so the burgers were technically not invented by you. You just redid what Hunter created." She wasn't taking this conversation seriously, and I tried to hold back a laugh. "Means...you like Hunter's cooking better than mine. I get it. It's settled." I shrugged, letting her take both plates. I opened a drawer, picked up two forks, and put them next to each slice on the plates.

A grin spread on her face, and by shaking her head she let me know that she understood that I wasn't serious, either. "Come on, I really need to try this cake." She walked back to the living room, and I opened the fridge to check if there was something other to drink than water. "Beer or wine?" I called out, wondering why there was a bottle of red wine in the fridge if Harlow wasn't allowed to drink, or drank alcohol at all, and Hunter preferred beer over any other alcoholic drink. *Maybe they received it as a present*, I thought.

"Wine sounds good," Gray answered, and I grabbed the bottle out of the fridge, then looked for

149

some wine glasses but only found regular ones and took them back to the couch Gray was sitting on. I sat down next to her and filled both glasses halfway. "I've never heard of this wine, but it's definitely not an expensive one."

"It's wine." She shrugged, then lifted her glass and looked me in the eyes. "As long as it fulfills its purpose, I don't care how cheap it is." I was in on that as well. Although, I did prefer beer.

"You're right," I told her and raised my glass as well. "To us," I offered, and Gray nodded.

"And to this beautiful cake that is ready for me to devour," she added with a grin. We both took a sip of the wine, and I was surprised by how good it tasted. I put the glass down, then reached for the plate. Gray did the same, and I waited for her to take the first bite to tell me if she liked it. I watched her closely, and the second she put the first piece of cake into her mouth, her eyes widened.

"Oh, my God," she moaned, and I chuckled because I knew exactly how delicious Harlow's cakes tasted.

"Right?"

She nodded quickly, pointed at the cake on the plate with her fork. "This…is the best thing I've ever had. We need to get more tomorrow." She ate another piece, and I enjoyed watching her eat. So, I leaned back, my plate still in my hand and my eyes fixated on hers for a second before I started eating myself.

"You still wanna hear about Bliss?" I asked, putting my plate down when I was finished with my cake.

Gray nodded, putting her plate on top of mine and pulling her knees up to get comfortable.

"If you're okay with letting me in on that story, of course." I nodded at her words, then ran a hand through my hair to prepare myself for what I was about to tell.

"I've known Bliss since I was seventeen, I think. As Hunter's sister, we've often seen each other around his home and the town. But we've never really spoken up until almost exactly one year ago. A few months before Hunter and Harlow even started seeing each other, I was out one night at a bar. I just left work and needed a drink and I had some things on my mind I had to clear up before going back home to Harlow." Before I continued the story, I could see that exact night flash through my mind, and I recalled every single second from that evening.

March 3rd, 2019

"You look lonely," a familiar voice said behind me, and I turned my head to meet her eyes. I smiled at Bliss, taking in her pretty face.

"Wanna keep me company?" I suggested, then nodded to the stool next to me. I didn't mind Bliss, but I'd never thought of her as a friend. Until now. "Want a drink?" I asked, watching her sit down next to me and smile as I made the offer.

"I'm good, thanks. You don't come here often, right?" I shook my head and took a sip of my bourbon.

"Not too often. Didn't think I would meet you here someday. How's life?"

I wasn't a big talker, and I didn't really care what others were up to. The only person I talked to a lot and cared deeply about was Low, and sometimes Hunter when it was necessary. Other people didn't interest me much, and I had nothing to say to them. With girls, I liked to get their names, go back to their place, fuck, and then leave as soon as possible. I didn't flirt to get to know girls better. I flirted to get in their pants, and yes...that's the biggest asshole move ever. But committing to anyone wasn't in my schedule. And to be fair, I didn't get with many girls. Maybe one every three weeks.

Bliss shrugged. "Work's okay. Just moved into a new apartment. It's closer to the diner, but further from Hunter. I worry about him sometimes, and he doesn't let me help him."

I nodded because I knew about Hunter's mental health issues. The first time I met him he was all tough and intimidating, and his words had a way of scaring people. Now that I knew him better, I was able to keep him safe from himself and the dangers he often put himself in. But I wasn't talking to his sister about his health.

"He's doing okay. Saw him this morning. He came by my work and I checked his car. I'll take care of him, B. Don't worry."

Bliss knew about Hunter's job, and what he did to earn his money, but I wasn't sure she knew that I did just the same. I didn't care, though.

"I'm glad he has you. He doesn't really listen to me anyway." Bliss stopped, then studied my face carefully and smiled mischievously. "Do you think

he would care about us having a little fun? You look like you could use some. And I happen to have time tonight." Many girls switched the way Bliss just did. One second, they were all serious and caring, the next they wanted to take me to bed and show me a good time. I finished my drink, then looked at the time on my phone.

"I'd love to, Bliss, but maybe another night. I need to get home to Low." I didn't think it was a good idea to sleep with my friend's sister. I would kill Hunter if he tried anything with Low. Getting up from my stool, I put some money on the counter and looked back at her. "I'll see you around."

"So…you didn't go to bed with her that night?" Gray asked, her head now propped up against her hand, and her elbow leaning on the back of the couch. I shook my head, then continued to talk. "Bliss gave me her number that night. Wrote it down on a napkin and pushed it into my pocket. Long story short…we met up a few days later, had sex, and since Bliss wasn't into one-night stands, she offered me to come over whenever I needed some relief."

Gray kept listening, and she never showed any sign of jealousy or disgust. I was glad she understood because the rest of the story was a little more complicated. "We kept this sex-as-friends-thing up for weeks, and I never felt like I was doing something wrong until she started shouting and screaming, even hitting me and telling me that I only used her for my pleasure. I didn't understand her reason at the beginning, but it quickly hit me when she asked me if I even cared about her." I sighed, bracing myself for what I was going to say next. "She was way ahead of me, thinking we were heading toward a relationship with each other. The funny thing is, we never talked about it. She never mentioned anything about her feelings, but always ordered me to fuck her and then leave."

"I think she was confused..." Gray suggested, her eyes understanding and her voice calm. "Things like that happen a lot. I've heard so many stories about girls having these friends with benefits things going on, and then falling for the guy who only agreed to sex with no strings attached," she told me. "I think there was a lack of communication between you two."

I nodded and was glad she wasn't holding anything against me or Bliss. "I think you've said enough about your past. I wanna enjoy the time with you."

I agreed with that. In the end, Gray and I both knew what we had was deeper than my story with Bliss. Gray knew how I felt about her, and I knew she felt the same toward me.

CHAPTER TWENTY-SIX

Gray

The next morning, I woke up to loud thunder and heavy rain. When I opened my eyes to look at the time on my phone, I was surprised by how early I woke up. It was only five twenty a.m., and I wasn't tired at all. Instead of trying to fall back asleep, I thought cuddling up to Jagger and enjoying the moment was a better idea. His arms were around me, my back pressed against him and our legs tangled. I slowly turned in his embrace, making sure not to move too much so I didn't wake him. Once I was facing him, a tired smile appeared on his lips.

"Can't sleep?" he murmured, then opened his eyes to look into mine. I nodded, then smiled back at him because the sight of him with messy hair from our make-out last night made my heart flutter. He was so damn handsome.

"I think it's the weather," I whispered, nestling my face into the crook of his neck. I breathed in his scent, then kissed the spot right under his jawline.

Jagger's hands moved up my back, and one of them grabbed a fistful of my hair while the other settled on my lower back. "I somehow missed it. It's comforting. And now holding you in my arms with the rain pouring outside makes it even better." His voice was raspy and thick from sleep, and I felt the vibrations on his neck while he spoke.

I kept my face buried and moved my hand up his bare stomach and chest, feeling his muscles under my touch all over again. I liked being close to him like this. But there was something holding me back from moving my hand down to his boxer briefs and continuing what we started last night. I was still thinking about the story he told me with Bliss and him. But it wasn't Bliss that bothered me…it was Hunter.

"Can I ask you something?" I lifted my head to look down at him, my head propped up on my hand.

"Anything," he whispered, brushing his hand through my hair.

"As you told the story about you and Bliss, you said something about working with Hunter and how he sometimes would be in danger or put himself in bad situations…" I didn't know how to continue or what to ask. It all sounded dark, but I might've misunderstood something.

Jagger studied my face, and I knew he was thinking about how to put whatever he was going to say. I let him think, not rushing him or trying to push him to say something he was uncomfortable sharing. Jagger mentioned Hunter having mental health issues, and I knew that topic was difficult for many people. I never had to deal with anyone who had any problems, but I knew that if a close friend of mine ever had issues with something, I would help and support them, so if Jagger wasn't ready to talk about it, I would understand and step back.

"It's not easy to explain," he said, and I saw the fight he was having with himself about trying to figure out what to say. But I knew he wanted to tell me more. "I'm not getting into details, and I don't want you to think wrong of Hunter and me. It's in our past. I'm not proud of what I did, and I can only speak for myself. But Hunter's not a bad person or else I would have never let him be with Low."

I nodded quickly, letting him know that I wasn't going to judge him for what he chose to do when he was younger. I was happy that he opened up to me, though. I'd seen something in his eyes lately. Since the day he asked me to come here to visit his sister, there was hurt flashing through his eyes. Not too often, though, and I was lucky enough to get a glance of that emotion.

"Both of you are incredible guys. He's slightly intimidating," I chuckled, "but I saw how happy Harlow was with him and the love they have for each other can be felt in this house without them being here. And you...you're incredibly kind, Jagger. I trust you."

He smiled and leaned in to kiss me. When his lips left mine again, I smiled back at him and waited for him to continue. "Hastings isn't the safest place to grow up. Especially this area and the trailer park Hunter lived at. When I first came here with Harlow, I was lucky enough to get this house and get a roof above her head. Then, a few years after I

started my first job at the mechanic's, I met Hunter
and he got me into some illegal stuff. We...dealt
around town and shit like that. I knew it wasn't
right since getting caught could make me lose
Harlow, but I soon found out that I was good at it,
especially with Hunter by my side. He's a crazy
sonofabitch...but we were safe with each other." He
stopped, and I held in my breath and wondered why
I wasn't getting mad or scared. Probably because I
couldn't imagine Jagger as a dealer. Or doing illegal
things altogether. What stuck with me was the way
he cared about Harlow. How he cared about her
before he even thought of himself.

"We got into some other things. I'm not that
comfortable sharing with you or anyone, for that
matter, but I'll say this much..." He took in a deep
breath, not taking his eyes off mine and gripping the
back of my hair tight, but not to the point that it
hurt. "I'm never going back there. It was a dark
fucking place and I'm glad I'm out of it. I'm happy
Hunter is taking care of Low, and I'm glad I live in
Newton now, where the most incredible girl I've
ever met lives. I'm happy. They're happy. That's all
that counts." The honesty he said that with hit deep
in the heart. I didn't care what he did before I met
him, and I wasn't going to bring it up ever.

"I hope you still wanna be here with me. I don't
think I can let you go this quick," he added, and I
immediately shook my head to let him know that I
wasn't going anywhere.

"You'd have to have killed people to make me
run from you. I see the man you are today, Jagger,"
she promised, then kissed his lips gently.

Jagger

Her answer scared the shit out of me. Not only had she triggered something I told myself never to think about again, but she literally said what I've been doing all those years before moving to Newton. *Fuck!*

I was keeping it a secret, and secrets were okay as long as they didn't harm the people we loved. But this secret was big. I wanted to tell her. I wanted her to know everything about me so she wouldn't find out later in life and hate me. I couldn't tell her, though. She didn't know life as I had. Or Hunter. She would be scared as hell. Maybe even call the damn cops on me. But I couldn't let that happen.

Just ignore it. It's in the past. You've moved on, Goddammit!

Her kiss was an easy distraction. The way her lips moved against mine was soothing, yet exciting. I pushed all the bad thoughts aside and pushed myself up to lay her on her back. I leaned over her, kissing her deeper now. My tongue moved inside her mouth with ease, touching hers and making a soft moan escape her.

"I want you, Jagger," she whispered into the kiss. I was hesitant at first. I knew once I was inside her, it was over for me. No other girl would make me feel this way and I had to decide if I wanted to live with this unclear conscience until she eventually found out all about my past as a hitman.

CHAPTER TWENTY-SEVEN

Gray

I felt his hardness pressing against my middle. I was already aching for him, and the heat made it obvious that I was ready for him. The last time I had sex was when I was twenty, and two years is a long time to remember what it felt like. My last time was horrible. The guy I was seeing at the time was selfish and didn't care what I liked, in bed and life in general. The weirdest thing was that every time we were about to have sex, he wanted reassurance that his dick was big enough. Obviously, he knew it was, but he wanted me to say it out loud to boost his ego. Also, while giving him blowjobs, he challenged me to find out how deep I could take it in. After I stopped seeing him, I reminded myself that I didn't need a guy in my life to feel something. I began to feel happier without him or any other guy. My decision not to date anymore made me less insecure.

With Jagger, everything was different. It's not

that I was happier when he was around, or that I wasn't content with myself when I was alone, but he added to all the positive things in life. I found myself thinking about him more and more, and after our first date, I knew I wasn't going to push him out of my mind that quickly.

"Take these off," I mumbled against his lips and tugged on his briefs. He immediately lifted his hips, then stopped our kiss and looked into my eyes. For a moment, I thought he would end what we started, but then he grinned.

"Bossy little thing," he teased, then got off the end of the bed and stood there, looking down at me still lying on my back. "I want you to do it," he commanded, and I found myself sitting up quickly. I wasn't much into men bossing *me* around, but with Jagger, it was exciting.

I moved toward the end of the bed, now kneeling in front of him. We were eye to eye, and I looked down at the bulge growing in his briefs. My right hand moved down his stomach, and my eyes met his again. There was lust written all over his face, and my desire for him grew, knowing how much he wanted this too.

Jagger watched me closely while my hand moved down to his cock, and I decided that I didn't want it covered any longer. I pushed one side of the briefs down, then helped myself with my other hand and pulled it down fully, revealing his length.

He was fully erect, and I couldn't stop myself from putting my hand around the base of it, then moving it up and down before looking back up at Jagger. His eyes were still on my face, and his hands reached out to touch my hips.

"Fuck," he breathed out as I started pumping my hand along his length faster. I smiled, knowing I was making him feel good. There was no pressure from either of us and I liked the control he let me have. "Does this feel good?" I asked, knowing exactly how much he liked it.

He chuckled, then squeezed my bottom and pulled me closer. "You have no fucking idea. Lay back," he ordered, leaving a trail of kisses down my neck.

"No," I shot back, and the way his hands tightened on my ass told me that he wasn't okay with that answer.

"Gray," he murmured against my skin, then moved the shirt I was wearing up to my waist, with his hands lingering there. "Lay back," he repeated, but I didn't move. His cock was still in my hand, and I stopped as my fingers touched the tip of it where precum was already coming out.

"I wanna touch you some more," I told him, putting my left hand on the back of his head, and pulling him back so he had to look at me. "Let me." The desire in his eyes grew. I think he wasn't used to women being in control. I knew he wanted to be the one ordering me around and telling me what to do, but I had my own things I wanted to do to. With my eyes stuck on his, I moved back on my knees, then leaned down so my head was right in front of his cock.

"Gray, you don't have to," he panted.

"I want to," was all I said before my tongue licked along his tip, immediately tasting the saltiness of his precum. "Fuck…" Jagger groaned and grabbed a handful of my hair. I looked up at him, and he was watching me still.

I didn't want to tease him, so I covered his tip with my lips, then moved them down his length, taking him deeper into my mouth. Somehow, when a guy wasn't telling me what to do, it was more fun. So, I moved faster, my hand still at the base of his cock and moving simultaneously with my mouth.

"Ah, fuck, baby. Just like that." His words were still thick with sleep and the rain outside made this whole situation somehow romantic. It was dark, but not dark enough to see each other. I kept going, feeling the veins on his cock pulsate, and his hand tugged on my hair tighter.

"My turn," he suddenly said and grabbed my neck with his other hand to pull me back up on my knees. His lips found mine, and the kiss he gave me almost made me swoon. The passion with which he moved his lips against mine and the way his tongue swirled around mine made me ache even more down there.

He pushed me back, making me fall back on the mattress. He moved quickly over me, pulling my panties down my legs with ease. "I want a taste too." A grin appeared on his face and I couldn't help myself from laughing. I was excited, and my head was already spinning. I could tell by the way he touched and kissed me that I was in for a treat with him between my legs. Not many guys excited me the way he did, and since I couldn't wait to feel him between my legs, I pushed against his shoulders.

"Someone's needy." He chuckled, and I nodded to let him know how much I wanted it.

"Please," I whispered, then quickly felt a trail of kisses going down my stomach. He pushed my legs apart, kissing the inside of my left thigh gently. His tongue came out, licking the spot he'd just kissed, then moved further up. My hand gripped his full head of hair, pulling at the ends slightly.

"Jagger, please…" I moaned, trying to move his head in the right direction, but he wasn't done teasing me. One of his hands moved under my bottom, holding it tight and lifting my hips slightly. His other hand held my thigh, making it hard for me to move. Then, finally, I felt his tongue between my folds, up until he finally reached that little nub I was desperate for him to lick.

Once he got there, he flicked his tongue against it like he had never done anything else before. My whole body started to shiver, and I kept his head right in that spot to make sure he wouldn't stop. Lucky for me, he kept going.

"Oh, God," I moaned, and I felt the tension inside of me rising. I wanted to let go, but what he was doing to me felt too good to just let it end that quickly. I held on to whatever was keeping me from climaxing.

"Come for me, Gray." Jagger's voice was demanding, and I knew I had to let go sooner or later. I did, and the orgasm spreading through my whole body made me shake and wish for him to do it all over again. But that wasn't the case. Jagger moved back over me, his right hand covering my folds and massaging my clit to keep the feeling of the orgasm up for a little while longer.

"You okay?" he asked, almost out of breath, and I nodded, smiling up at him.

"Yes," I answered, grabbing his face between my hands, and pulling him down to kiss him. I didn't care about my own taste on his lips, and I let my tongue dance with his.

I felt his cock on my belly now, and I reached down with one hand to move it where I wanted it to be. Jagger broke the kiss and looked at me with concern in his eyes. "Let me get a condom, sweetheart."

I nodded and watched him get up from the bed. He walked toward the bedroom door, and I frowned, wondering where he was going. Before he left the room, he turned with a crooked grin. "Gotta check in Hunter's room. I don't have any with me."

As I waited on him to come back, I smiled at the thought of Jagger not thinking about sex while coming to Hastings. It was a bit of a weird situation for him to grab condoms in his sister's room, but since she was already pregnant, Hunter could probably spare some protection for us.

Jagger came back with a little square foil in his hand, and I smiled at the sight of his naked body, standing right in front of the bed. He smirked, then opened the foil and pulled the condom over his hard cock. I watched him carefully, not wanting to miss any second of it. As a chuckle escaped his chest, I looked back up to his face and felt my cheeks heat up immediately. "Next time, I wanna watch you do it."

He climbed back on the bed, then leaned over me

with each hand on one side of my head to hold himself up. His knees pushed mine aside, and he positioned himself between my legs. The tip of his cock touched my entrance, and I got more excited when he slowly started pushing against it.

"Tell me what you like, Gray." His eyes were on mine, and even if I felt like closing my eyes to enjoy the feeling even more, I couldn't keep my eyes off his.

"Go slow," I whispered. "Let me get used to you first."

He nodded and bent down to kiss the corner of my mouth softly. I knew it wasn't going to be easy to push inside me, considering not only his length but also his width. He reached down between us to direct the tip to my entrance, and I spread my legs wider, so it was easier for him to get there. With one slow push, I felt him fully inside me. The pain quickly vanished, and I adjusted myself underneath him to get myself and him more comfortable.

"You can move," I told him, but I feared the first pumps inside me because I knew I had yet to get used to him inside me.

Jagger kept his eyes on me, making sure I wasn't hurting. His hips started to move, and I held my breath for a few seconds before realizing how good it felt.

"Faster," I moaned, and Jagger didn't think twice. His thrusts increased, and I felt him plunge deeper inside me.

"Fuck," he groaned, and I grabbed a fistful of his hair to pull him back down. I kissed his lips, and he opened his mouth to dip his tongue inside my mouth. Jagger kept moving fast, and one of his hands wrapped around my throat, gripping just enough so I was still able to breathe. It felt good, and as he broke the kiss once again, he tilted my head to the side to kiss my neck.

"Jagger, please," I said breathlessly. "Harder…"

"Fuck, baby. Anything for you." And that's when he started moving even faster, but this time, with each thrust, a loud moan escaped me. He wasn't holding back, and I was enjoying it a little too much. I didn't want this to end, but just like myself, his cock started pulsating. I knew he was close, and all I wanted was for him to get the same relief I did just minutes before.

"I want you to come inside me." I was out of breath, but he heard what I said clearly. Another groan escaped him, and he kept his pace up. Jagger moved up, now kneeling, and kept going without a pause. His hands gripped my hips tightly, and he pulled me into his thrusts each time.

"Come," he ordered, and just when another wave hit me, I let go, and I felt him do the same. He stopped moving, and the throbbing of his cock inside me was enough for me to know that he came too.

Speechless from what just happened, I closed my eyes and took deep breaths. "Fuck…" he murmured, then I felt him lean over me once again and kissing my lips gently. I didn't move but enjoyed the intimacy between us.

It was still pouring outside, and silent thunders could be heard in the distance. "You make me so fucking happy," he whispered into the kiss, and I smiled, but I couldn't build real words just yet.

CHAPTER TWENTY-EIGHT

Jagger

After a long hot shower, Gray and I both got dressed to drive back to the diner, so I could finally sign the papers I initially came to Hastings for. The drive to Frankie's was quiet, but we both smiled at each other multiple times, not able to hide how much we enjoyed our first time. It was incredible, and Gray stunned me with her openness. She was vocal when it came to sex, and I was glad she spoke up about what she liked and what she didn't like. It made it easier for me because I sure as hell wasn't going to hold back seeing her naked on my bed with that beautiful body of hers.

We arrived at our destination, and I parked the car next to Hunter's. With our seatbelts off, we both got out, and Gray walked around the car to stand beside me.

"I'm up for pancakes. This morning made me hungry," she told me with a grin. I chuckled, locking my car, and pushing the key into my pocket. "Me too. Come on."

I grabbed her hand and slid my fingers through hers to keep her close. Somehow, just having her next to me wasn't enough. I needed physical reassurance that she wouldn't walk away out of the blue, which was stupid to think about. Still, touching her made me feel secure. And I wanted her to feel protected.

Pulling the door open, I let her enter first, then stepped in behind her and let the door slam shut again. With a glance around the diner, there wasn't much space left to sit. People were enjoying their coffee and breakfasts, and all the smells mixed made my mouth water.

"Let's check over there," I said with a nod toward the other end of the row of booths. I knew Hunter was in the back cooking, but I couldn't see Harlow anywhere. Even though Hunter didn't want her to work too much, I couldn't imagine my sister *not* working on a busy morning like this.

As we approached the other end, I saw Harlow sitting in the booth in the far corner, facing our direction. She wasn't alone. She was talking to someone sitting opposite her, and the second I saw the silver hair, I knew who my sister was with. I was ready to turn back around and walk straight back to my car, but I didn't want to look weak.

"There's Harlow," Gray pointed out, not knowing that Bliss was sitting there too. Harlow noticed us and smiled. There was no sign of worry in her eyes, and I wasn't starting any drama for her sake. Bliss's head turned, and I braced myself for the look she would give me after not seeing me in

170

weeks. We left on good terms, yes. But with Bliss, you never knew.

Her expression was friendly until her eyes moved to Gray standing next to me. Taking my eyes off Bliss, I looked down at Gray. "Bliss is here," I stated, knowing she already noticed her. "You okay with that?" She finally tore her gaze from Bliss and Harlow's direction.

"Why wouldn't I be?" Her voice was soft. Soothing, in a way. She wasn't nervous about the situation, but I sure as fuck was.

"You two didn't have a great start back then. I know how she can get," I told her, but Gray shrugged it off and nudged me into their direction. "Come on, I'm hungry."

Gray was the one pulling me toward the booth, and as we stopped in front of it, Harlow got up and hugged her tight. "Good to see you again," Harlow said cheerfully, then leaned back to look Gray in the eyes. "Did you have a good first night in Hastings?"

"It was perfect. I really enjoyed your cake," she informed Low. I let the two of them talk.

To not stand there and feel awkward, I looked down at Bliss and gave her a tight smile. "You doing okay?" I asked, and she got up, putting her arms around my neck to greet me. I patted her back, then hoped for her to get off me again. Somehow, since knowing Gray, I wasn't comfortable with other women touching me. Other than Low, of course.

"I'm great," she announced, finally letting go of me. I found myself reaching for Gray the second my hand was free again, but since I couldn't just pull her from talking to Harlow, I rested my hand on her lower back. "You've got company, I see." Bliss nodded toward Gray, not shifting her eyes from mine though. I nodded, then turned to look over to the other two talking. I caught their attention by clearing my throat, and both looked at me.

"Gray, this is Bliss. You two have met briefly." I didn't say more since there was nothing else to declare.

I braced myself for the worst, because the last time they saw each other, Gray provoked Bliss by putting my arm around her shoulders while I walked her back home. I knew Gray's intentions weren't bad, but I knew Bliss. She got triggered by the littlest things.

For a moment, I wasn't sure any of them were going to talk, but then Gray smiled apologetically. "I remember. I wish that night would've gone a little smoother. I was a bitch, and I'm sorry about that."

That's a start, I thought. But it wasn't over yet. By the look of Bliss's expression, she was thinking about what Gray had said, and was deciding how to take her apology.

"It's all good. I don't think I would've reacted any differently than you did." And with that, they hugged it out and a weight was lifted from my shoulders. At least they weren't going to sit in silence and make breakfast awkward. "This guy's a keeper. You got lucky," Bliss added, and it sounded genuine. *Well, that's new.*

I smiled at Gray, moving my hand back to her waist. "We're both pretty hungry. Is Hunter still making pancakes?"

Harlow nodded and moved out of the booth so Gray and I could sit down. "Bliss and I will eat as well. I'll go grab the papers so it's off our minds."

Before she left, Gray reached out to touch Harlow's belly. "You're already showing. You're gorgeous…" she said in awe, and after Gray pointing it out, I realized how Harlow's belly showed signs of her pregnancy in the dress she was wearing. I'd not seen her in skirts and dresses often, but it looked good on her with the matching tights and boots.

Harlow frowned, touching her belly now. "I feel bloated. Someone's asked me if I gained some pounds, and they didn't believe me when I told them I had a baby in there." Her voice was sad, but I knew she wasn't taking it seriously.

"You look great, sweet girl. You're the prettiest mama I've ever seen and the baby's not even out yet," I assured her, which made her smile.

"Thanks, but you have to say that." Harlow laughed, then left our table.

"She's doing great. I've never seen Hunter smile that much in my life. I'm glad she's keeping him down to earth," Bliss said, smiling at Gray and me. "And how are you two lovebirds doing?"

I glanced over at Gray, and I was more than happy to answer that question, even if Bliss was the one to ask. "She's amazing. I don't wanna rub it in your face…but I think I've found the one." I hoped to lighten the mood even more but also tried to challenge Bliss at the same time. Not sure why I wanted that, but a small voice inside my head told me to do it.

Bliss nodded, then leaned back and sighed. "I think we're heading the same direction then. I've met a guy. Tall, dark, handsome as hell. He's the new president of Hastings College, and I would lie if I said that we didn't have sex in one of the classrooms yet."

And there it was. The weird side I was expecting to pop up once she got a little too comfortable. She wanted to let me know just how well she was doing without me, and honestly, good for her. Her moving on meant that I had nothing to worry about anymore. She found a new toy and she would play with it until she got bored again.

"Is that allowed?" Gray asked. She had a point, but then, I didn't care what Bliss did with other men. I squeezed Gray's thigh, making her squirm next to me. The reaction I got from her just from touching her made me want to pick her up and get out of here, to drive back home and do what we did just a little over an hour ago all over again.

Bliss shrugged with a smug grin on her face. "Don't really care. We're happy. That's what's important, right?" Gray and I nodded simultaneously, and I was glad Harlow was back with a small binder in her hands. "All right, the pancakes will be ready soon." Bliss moved over to let Harlow sit down opposite of me, and I reached for the binder and pen Low put on the table. "It's the first document. It just states that Hunter will be the owner of the house once you've signed."

I was already reading the first few lines, then skipped some words to get to the last line where my signature would go. "And you're sure you don't wanna be the owner? What if you guys fight and you don't have anywhere to go?"

Harlow's brows were furrowed, tighter than I've ever seen them before. "Don't you dare say things like that." She tried to sound angry, but she looked rather adorable with that face. I laughed it off, then signed the paper and pushed it back to her. "It's just a thought, Low."

"Keep it to yourself." Harlow's feistiness grew day by day, and I liked it. She was getting stronger, defending herself and speaking up when something bothered her. I was proud, knowing she was turning into a confident young woman. She was happy, and that's all that mattered.

CHAPTER TWENTY-NINE

Gray

"So, when are you guys heading back to Newton?" Bliss asked, eating the last strawberry from her plate. Hunter was now sitting at the booth too. He squeezed in next to Harlow, who looked rather squashed between Hunter and Bliss. She didn't seem to mind, so I didn't bother asking about it.

"Tomorrow. Gray's got to get back to work in the afternoon. And I might ask Dallas if he needs me tomorrow at the bar." The last sentence was directed to me, and I looked up at Jagger and nodded.

"I think he'd be thrilled. He likes you quite a bit," I grinned.

"Who's Dallas?" Harlow asked. She was already done eating her pancakes and now leaned into Hunter's side to get more comfortable. His arm came around her shoulders, and he pulled her closer.

"Dallas is my brother. He owns a club in town and offered Jagger a job. He's done great so far. Dallas is fascinated by him, I think."

"He's not fascinated." Jagger laughed, then looked at Hunter. "Her brother is Dallas Washington. Remember that guy everyone wanted to fight years back? I wasn't ready to take on a guy like him, so now he thinks he's better than me because he made it much further in the MMA business."

Hunter chuckled, shaking his head. "No fucking way. I wanted to take him on myself, and I didn't even do those stupid cage fights." He then swung his gaze to me and smiled. "Heard a lot about your brother. Sounds like a nice guy."

I nodded quickly, then scrunched my nose. "He's taking it a little too far lately. I want him to stop fighting, but he just won't listen. He's not in the greatest shape anymore."

I saw Harlow look down at her hands, and Jagger patted my thigh to signal me not to talk about underground fights anymore. My lips parted, then shut tightly so I wouldn't continue talking about my brother.

"I'm sorry. I didn't mean to upset you, Harlow." I knew the story about Jagger and Harlow's time back in the days when Harlow found out about Jagger fighting and wanting him to stop. Jagger had told me that she often watched him come home with bloody noses and bad bruises, and lucky for her, he stopped once he realized how upset Harlow got seeing him like that.

"No, it's fine," Low said calmly. She looked

back up at me, then over at her brother. "I wish Jagger knew better back then. Fighting like that can leave physical damage, and I really hope your brother one day sees that too." She smiled now, looking back at me with a soft expression.

"I think you're all overreacting. Guys who fight in cages with only boxing shorts on is hot. I gotta see one of Dallas's fights. You gotta get me his number, Gray." Bliss's words surprised me, and to be fully honest, I didn't like the thought of her in a room with my brother. Not because I didn't want them to get to know each other, but because they were too damn similar—both loud and very hyper, and knowing my brother, he wouldn't hold back on a woman like Bliss. Even though she was gushing over her new man just minutes ago, there was something about her carelessness that didn't match up with her words.

"Right, I think you're good for now, sis." Hunter slid out of the booth and got up, then helped Harlow stand up as well. "Take care of that college guy first, then Gray can let you meet her brother." He winked at me, and I smiled to thank him for his help. I wouldn't have known what to say to Bliss, so I was glad Hunter spoke up for me.

"Come say goodbye tomorrow morning before you leave, all right? I'll make you some sandwiches to eat on your way back to Newton." While he spoke, Hunter started to take our dishes off the table to bring them back to the kitchen.

"Thanks, man. We will," Jagger said, then reached out to grab Harlow's hand. "You okay?"

Harlow nodded, then bent down to kiss Jagger's

cheek. "See you tomorrow, all right?" She then looked at me and smiled. "Have a nice day. Let Jagger take you around Hastings. There are some nice places to visit."

And with that, they left our table with the plates in their hands. I moved my eyes back to Jagger, and I saw him looking at Bliss.

"I gotta leave too. I start work in two hours, and I need to get ready at home." She slid over the bench to get up, and Jagger seemed to relax next to me.

"Drop by work tomorrow so I can say goodbye too. You have to drive by it anyway."

"Okay, see you tomorrow," Jagger answered, but didn't move. Bliss was obviously waiting for him to get up and hug her, so I nudged his side, and with a sigh, he got up to give a proper goodbye. I didn't want to seem rude, and I genuinely hoped for her and me to get along well. I hugged her goodbye too. "It was nice spending some time with you, Bliss."

"Same," she simply said, then moved back to look at us again. "Tomorrow. Don't forget," she warned Jagger, then she left the diner.

"Jesus Christ," I heard Jagger whisper under his breath, and I couldn't help a chuckle.

"Oh, come on, Jagger. That wasn't so bad."

"You have no idea," he growled, running his hands through his hair. "It's like she's the same person, but more annoying than before."

"She's not trying to annoy you, though. Just trying to push you out of her mind. Why else would she talk about her new man like that? I like her," I said honestly, but I did have to get used to her first.

"I need some fresh air," Jagger announced, which made me laugh.

"You're overreacting. Come on. Show me around town so you can get your mind off her," I suggested.

"Good idea."

And so we left the diner, both with bellies full of pancakes and fruit, and ready to go for a little walk before heading back home.

CHAPTER THIRTY

Jagger

Showing Gray all the places I liked in Hastings didn't take long. There wasn't much to see. The only places I enjoyed hanging out at were Frankie's Diner, the mechanic's I worked, and my own home. After all the things that happened in this town, I didn't find much happiness in other areas. Most of them reminded me of all the jobs I received from Gunner, hunting down men, and killing them. Thinking back…that wasn't my greatest time in life. I'd harmed a lot and earned crazy amounts of money for doing something so wrong.

In the end, it helped Harlow and me out of our misery. The demons I carried with me to Newton were slowly disappearing, but with Gray becoming a bigger part of my life with each day that passed, guilt kept on building up inside me.

Keeping secrets from people you loved wasn't easy. I learned it the hard way with Harlow, but with her being the most kind-hearted and

181

understanding girl in the whole world, she was quick to forgive me. I got lucky having her as my sister, and so did Hunter, for being the love of her life. But Gray didn't grow up in a family where her brother killed for money. She didn't know about all the bad things that could happen with a drug addict as a father, and a mother who didn't show her face anymore after birthing her second child because alcohol was more important to her than family.

From what Gray had told me about her family, and as much as I had already seen from her relationship with her brother and cousin, she lived the picture-perfect life everyone ever dreamed of. I didn't want to be the one to ruin it for her and disappoint her after letting me near her. Everything she ever told me about her life was a step closer to her heart, and I was starting to slowly build the wall of trust between us.

"Are you okay in there?" Gray's voice came from outside the bathroom, in which I was standing in front of the mirror, staring at myself. I ran my hand through my hair and picked up my toothbrush.

"Yeah, I'll be with you in a second." I started brushing my teeth, then looked back into the mirror. My eyes looked empty, and I had to figure out how to handle the situation in which I was slowly sinking.

Gray's footsteps told me that she went back to the bedroom, and I hurried to meet her there. After putting my brush back, I washed my face and headed back to the bedroom.

"Everything okay?" Gray asked as I closed the door behind me and took off my shirt. I threw it on top of the dresser, then headed to the bed. She was sitting on the end, looking up at me as I approached her. With a smile, I cupped both her cheeks and bent down to kiss the tip of her nose.

"Just got some things on my mind," I told her in a whisper, my eyes steady on hers now. She was looking up with worry in her eyes, and that's when the voice inside my head told me to tell her all about my past. I was scared and unsure of how to go at it, though.

"Wanna talk about it?" Her voice was soft, which made it worse for me to talk. Gray was trying to figure me out by showing me how much she cared about me, and I wasn't blaming her. She knew there was something I was hiding, and it was the right thing to be suspicious. The look on her face said it all and it took all the strength I had to start talking.

But before I could say something, she got up from the bed and stood in front of me with her arms wrapped around my neck. "You know you can tell me anything, right? I'll listen," she stated, then stopped for a while to study my face. "I'm not pushing you to talk. Take your time, however much you need. I'll be here and ready to listen, all right?"

She gave me a way out, and I was thankful for that. It wasn't the right time to talk about my old life as a hitman. I had some things to figure out and the right words to find.

By the words she said just then, I felt my heart beat faster. I felt warm and the tingles in my chest made me realize that I had never felt like this for any other girl before. I was falling for her, quicker than I ever wished for.

"You're so fucking beautiful, inside and out." My lips touched hers, and she smiled into the kiss. I quickly picked her up to lay her back on the bed and moved over her to deepen our kiss.

With one elbow propped up on one side of her head, I somehow managed to pull down her slip, so I had easy access to her already wet pussy. I slowly ran my fingers through her folds, feeling just how excited she was. A moan escaped her, and I pushed my tongue deeper into her mouth.

When my fingers were drenched, I pushed them inside of her, making her arch her back. With her hips lifted, I moved my fingers in and out of her, gently at first, and then faster.

"You're so fucking tight, love," I groaned, now looking into her eyes while my fingers kept moving. Her eyes were fixated on mine, and her parted lips were a sign of pleasure. Another moan from her, and I pulled my fingers out of her.

"You're teasing me," she breathed, and I couldn't help a grin.

"Wouldn't be any fun if I didn't tease you, hm?"

She rolled her eyes at me, and even with a smile on her face, she was obviously annoyed. She was longing for me to keep stimulating her sweet pussy, and I was planning on doing just that. "I need you," she whispered, running her hands through my hair. "Now."

She wouldn't have to ask me twice. I pushed myself up on my knees, then pulled my briefs down to throw them to the ground. My dick was ready, and all I needed was to put a condom on and push myself inside of her. I was aching, and just like the night before, I was excited to be this close to her again.

I reached over to the nightstand, took one of the condoms and quickly opened it to pull it over my length. Gray watched the whole scene, her eyes never leaving my dick. I smirked, rubbing myself for her own pleasure.

"Enjoying yourself?" I asked, and she blushed after realizing that she was staring at me. Nodding, she sat up and was now close to my abdomen. Her hands came up and touched each side of my waist, then she ran them down my stomach, her eyes still on mine. "I think you're incredibly handsome..." she admitted. "But I guess you know that already."

I chuckled, watching her kiss my skin right next to my cock. Her hand moved over it at first, then her fingers wrapped around my length and moved up and down with just the right amount of pressure. I kept watching her until I had to stop myself from relaxing, and flexing whatever muscles were needed to hinder myself from coming too early. It was hard with Gray.

"If you want me to come inside of you again, I need you flat on your back and your legs spread so I can fuck that tight little pussy." With no hesitation, she leaned back. "I love how willing you are. Makes me want to fuck you over and over again," I drawled. Positioning myself between her legs, I grabbed my cock again and touched my tip to her entrance. With one swift move, I pushed inside of her, and the sensation overcoming me grew with each thrust.

"Promise to stay with me, no matter what," I breathed against her neck, nibbling on her skin, and licking the soft spot underneath her ear.

"I promise, Jagger," she moaned, and even though I never was the one who needed reassurance from anyone, I needed it from Gray now more than ever. I intended to keep her. For now, and hopefully forever.

CHAPTER THIRTY-ONE

Jagger

A week later and back in Newton, I started to get used to working at The Red. Those two women who wouldn't stop talking to me on my first night never showed up again, but Dallas talked about Chelsea a few times, saying how she couldn't wait for his next fight. He sounded slightly annoyed by her, even without her being present. I laughed it off and was grateful to have Gray around. Even if we didn't see each other for almost a week after returning, we texted a lot. Gray was busy painting, and I took up some extra shifts to make up for the missing three days we were in Hastings. I would see her again tonight, though.

It was Friday, March 13th, and it was Sage's birthday. She invited me this morning as I left for work at noon, and I promised her to show up with a present. I wasn't sure what to get her. I had no idea what she liked, besides cocktails and some occasional cigarettes to piss off her parents.

"You're coming tonight, right?" Dallas asked as he came around the bar to stand beside me. I was opening two beers for the guys in front of me and nodded to respond to his question. "Yeah. Any ideas on what I should get Sage? Don't really know her, and since she only just invited me this morning, I have limited time to find something good," I told him.

"Ah, don't worry about a present, man. I got a Jeroboam champagne bottle in the back. We'll just say it's from both of us. There are at least fifteen people giving her some sort of alcohol-related gift." He smirked. I knew what a Jeroboam was. It's basically a huge bottle which equals four normal-sized bottles, and it was the perfect gift for someone who liked to get drunk on a regular basis.

"Thanks," I said, sliding the beers over to the guys. As they left, I turned to Dallas. "So, you're also getting off at six? Do you need a ride?"

I knew he often jogged to work and took showers in his changing room downstairs. "Yeah, that'd be great. I'll just get my things and then we can leave. Levi and the rest will have their hands full tonight, and I don't wanna be around for that."

As the manager of the bar, you would think Dallas liked to be hands-on when guests came in to have a good time, but he'd much rather stay away from the hustle and hide either down in the cage, or in the back bothering his cooks and servers. I didn't mind leaving this place for the night either. Last night was rough, with a fucking frat party forming in here around eleven p.m. We had more drunks half an hour later than we would have in a whole week. We managed to get them out of here safely around one in the morning, and I was exhausted when I got home.

***

"I'll see you in ten," I told Dallas as he walked up the staircase with the champagne in his arms. I offered to help him, but he assured me that he wouldn't break it on the way up to Sage's apartment.

I walked into my apartment, already taking off my shirt, ready to take a quick shower to get rid of the cigarette smell from the bar, and then also head upstairs. Sage's party was already in full swing, with loud music playing and people laughing and singing along to the songs.

As I turned the corner to get to my bedroom, my front door opened again, and I swung back around. It wouldn't be the first time Dallas entered my apartment unannounced, but this time, it was his sister who disrespected any privacy rules.

"Hi," Gray said sweetly, closing the door behind her. She looked amazing. Her face was kept natural by the minimal makeup she put on, and her long, fiery hair was styled into big curls. The skirt she was wearing showed off her curves, but also her small waist. It reminded me of the outfit she wore on our first date at my place.

I chuckled. "Do the Washingtons not know how to knock or ring a bell?" I was mocking her, and her smile grew.

"No," she simply said and moved closer. Her

eyes fell to my chest, then lowered to my stomach where they stopped. "Why are you half-naked?"

"I need a shower. I smell like an ashtray dumped in a glass of scotch on the rocks." I reached out to cup the side of her neck, then pulled her closer. I was about to kiss her, but she moved her head back slightly to look up at me.

"Everyone smells like that upstairs." She shrugged, then her smile turned into a frown. "Please hurry. It's boring without you."

Another chuckle escaped me, and this time, she let me kiss her lips gently. Taking her in, I wrapped my arm around her back to keep her tight against my body. Her lips moved softly against mine, and my tongue quickly found a way to hers.

"I missed you," I whispered into the kiss before breaking it. We were still close, our foreheads touching while we tried to catch our breath. As I opened my eyes, I watched her keep hers closed, and after a pleased smile, she licked her lips. She did that a lot. Whenever I pulled back from a kiss, she stopped for a second to take in what just happened, making sure she remembered that certain feeling forever. On another note, I could tell she had already had one or two drinks by the taste on her tongue.

"I'll be ready in no time. Wait for me upstairs," I told her, and she nodded. Her eyes now opened, she slid her hands down my chest, lingering at my stomach. "Are you sure I can't watch you take a shower?" she asked, and this time I laughed.

"No, I am not. But I don't want to ruin the party by keeping the birthday girl's best friend and cousin away from her." I smirked, then took both her hands off my body and gave her a little pat on her bottom to signal her to move along. "I'll see you upstairs, beautiful."

Gray nodded in agreement, and with a small wave and adorable smile, she left my apartment. Had I known she was already here I would've hurried a little more when I got here. I intended on texting her after I took the shower, to ask her if she was on her way here, but then, she probably was here earlier than everyone else to help Sage set up the décor for the party.

I picked out a nice outfit and hopped in the shower to get rid of the smell and to quickly get upstairs to see Gray again.

CHAPTER THIRTY-TWO

Jagger

Just as I imagined, after I showered and got dressed to head upstairs, there was décor even in the hallway by Sage's floor. Two huge balloons in the form of the number 23 were floating right next to the door, and I had to duck to get inside without hitting them with my head.

The music was loud, and there were more guests now than there were at her last party a few weeks ago. I looked around the room to find someone I knew, but the only one I saw was Joey. As Sage's boyfriend, he probably knew where I could find her to congratulate her on getting a year older.

I moved through the crowd, finally reaching Joey, and putting my hand on his shoulder to get his attention.

"Jagger, right? What's up, man?" he said, and I was taken aback by the many girls he was surrounded by. They looked like they were all over him.

"Do you know where I can find Sage and Gray?" I didn't feel like talking much with him.

"Why?" A girl with a dress that was a hundred percent too small for her asked in an amused voice. I turned to look at her and lifted an eyebrow. *Don't be a dick, Jag.*

"Because it's Sage's birthday," I pointed out.

"Okay. But why are you looking for Gray?" she asked. The way she said Gray's name made me want to turn around and find them without anyone's help. She seemed annoyed, and she didn't even know me.

"She's my girl."

"Wow," was her response, and then her eyes moved from mine down my body, checking out every inch of me. It made me uncomfortable, and her behavior was incredibly annoying.

Ignoring her disgusted facial expression, I looked back at Joey, who was back flirting with another girl. "Never mind," I breathed and turned to walk back into the crowd and toward the kitchen.

As I reached it, I stopped in front of a large curtain that hung from one side of the arch to the other, hindering people from entering the once open kitchen. There wasn't much noise coming from it, so I figured it was the one space only Sage was allowed in. Other than that, I really could use some quiet time to prepare myself for the chaos in the living room.

I pulled the curtain aside and stepped into the kitchen. Luckily, both Gray and Sage were standing by the counter, decorating a large cake with melted chocolate and sprinkles.

"Looks good," I said, and they quickly turned to look at me.

Gray was quick to put down the bowl and walk over to me, her arms immediately wrapping around my neck and her lips pressing against my cheek. "Finally," she squealed happily, and I made a note in my head to make sure to monitor her drinking.

"Having fun, love?" I asked, and she nodded with no hesitation, and after a quick kiss to my lips, she went back to the cake. "I'm happy you're finally here with us. I missed you."

I smiled, eyeing her from behind. She was the sweetest, even when she was drinking. After admiring Gray, I turned to look at her cousin, who had a huge grin on her face.

"I should've placed a bet on you two. I knew there was a connection."

I chuckled, then stepped closer to hug her. "Happy birthday, Sage. Enjoying your party?" I asked and moved back to let her get back to decorating the cake.

"It's fun, yes. Who would've thought that Gray already had four more drinks than I did? Keep an eye on her tonight," she told me with a wink. I nodded, then leaned against the counter next to Gray.

My eyes wandered from the cake to her face, and her cheeks were already slightly pink from the alcohol. "Feeling okay?" I asked softly, brushing a strand of hair behind her ear. She looked at me with a smile, then pointed to the curtain behind me. "We're hiding in here. Joey brought some of his college friends and Sage wasn't happy about it.

We're decorating to distract her from him."

I looked over at Sage, whose expression was now sad, almost angry. "Want me to talk to him?"

"No. I'll just ignore him and tomorrow he'll be all over me again once those girls aren't around anymore." Sage's voice was sarcastic, and I knew it bothered her to see her boyfriend out there flirting with other girls.

"It's your birthday, Sage. You deserve to have fun, not hide in here and let him do what he does best. He's not caring much about the important thing tonight."

"He's right...maybe it's best if he talks to him. You know those girls will never leave if we tell them to. Let Jagger try," Gray suggested, looking at her cousin.

Sage sighed, then put her sprinkles down and looked back at me. "Okay, but if those girls don't leave, I will stay in this kitchen for the rest of the night."

I smiled tightly and looked back at Gray. "I'll be back."

Kicking someone out of an apartment that wasn't mine could get tricky. But I wanted Sage to have a great birthday, because everyone deserved to turn twenty-three while having fun, not hiding in the kitchen because her boyfriend was acting like a bachelor.

I stalked over to the group of girls surrounding Joey and tapped his shoulder to get his attention once again. He turned, but before he could say something, the girl from before moved closer to me with a grin.

"Did you miss me?" she tried to sound seductive and sexy, but all I heard was a frog who suddenly learned to speak.

"Fuck, no," I murmured and looked back at Joey. "Sage is upset. Any chance you can get rid of these girls so she can come out of the kitchen and have a nice birthday party?"

He laughed at my words. "She's just fine, man. She needs to relax a little. We're all just having fun."

"Right, everyone besides her." I sighed, looking at the girls around us, then back at Joey. "Can you at least come to talk to her for a second?" I asked in a low voice.

"Jesus, okay. Wait up, ladies. I'll be right back."

With Joey following me, we headed back to the kitchen. I held the curtain up so he could enter the room, and I stepped in behind him. Sage quickly looked at Joey, and there were high expectations in her eyes.

"Did you get rid of them?" she asked hopefully. Gray watched him closely.

"Why would I? We're just having fun. Come one, babe…don't be like that," Joey said, but those were the wrong words.

Sage stepped forward and pointed to the curtain behind Joey with a knife. I didn't notice it when I first came in, but the knife had some cake residue on it, probably from her cutting it before. "Then I'll get rid of you."

"I'll take this." I carefully took the knife out of her hand and put it on the counter to prevent any unwanted accidents. Then, Joey chuckled and shook his head. "The hell are you talking about? Come on, let's have some fun," he told her, but Sage wasn't having it.

"I'm done with you, Joey" was all she said before turning back to the cake. I looked at Gray, who was just as surprised as I was. But she also turned her back to Joey without a word.

"Are you fucking kidding me?"

I lifted an eyebrow, then nodded to the curtain. "Does she look like she is?" I asked him. "Get out, man."

With one last shake of his head, he left. Sage let out a relieved sigh, and I looked at her to make sure she was okay.

"Is there something I can get you?" I asked.

"Yes. The bottle of wine in my fridge, please. Thank you for helping, Jagger. I guess it was time to realize that he never treated me right the past few years…and he was terrible in bed," Sage admitted.

Gray and I looked at each other and laughed. "Fair reason to let someone go," I said under my breath and took out the bottle of wine Sage wished for. She didn't seem to be bothered much by the break-up. Good for her.

Chapter Thirty-Three

Gray

"Why did I just watch Joey leave with ten hot college girls?" Dallas asked as he entered the kitchen. He looked confused, and with Sage keeping quiet while eating cake, I was the one enlightening my brother.

"She broke up with him," I simply said, then looked over at Jagger, who was leaning against the fridge, drinking a beer. God, he looked so handsome. He didn't seem too bothered by what went on just minutes ago, and he kept calm the whole time.

"Hate to say it…but, finally." Dallas laughed and pulled Sage into an embrace.

"I thought you two were friends," Sage mumbled into his chest, and Dallas grimaced.

"He's annoying as shit. Only spent time with him because of you, Sage. Just because a family member has a boyfriend, doesn't mean I want to be friends with him."

"Ouch." Jagger frowned and put his hand over his chest, acting as if Dallas had just hurt his feelings. Dallas laughed and rolled his eyes.

"You're different, man. You don't annoy me, and you work for me. And I'm one hundred percent sure that you'd never be a dick like Joey and flirt with other girls at your girlfriend's birthday party."

I looked from Dallas to Jagger, and it might've been the alcohol, but something in me doubted what Dallas said. Jagger's eyes met mine, and a smile appeared on his lips. "She's the only one, even if she looks like she doesn't trust me right now." He chuckled and moved closer to me. He cupped my face with his hands and forced me to look into his eyes.

"I don't like what alcohol does to you, Gray," he whispered.

For a moment, I got lost in his eyes, and the words swirling around in my head didn't form real sentences. "I…"

Jagger raised an eyebrow, waiting for me to say something. There was a glimpse of amusement on his face, and I kept trying to build a grammatically correct sentence.

"Lost your voice there, Rusty?" Dallas's words sounded muffled, and I heard Sage giggle. They were still in the kitchen with us, but my attention span shrunk with each second, and all I saw was Jagger. My head was spinning, and I wondered if that last glass of vodka mixed with some soda was too much.

"You okay, love?" Jagger sounded concerned, and the crease between his brows deepened.

"Love," I repeated his last word spoken, and my heart suddenly started pumping faster, making me feel scared and excited at once. *What the hell is going on?*

"I love you." And then, everything went black

***

I heard voices from afar, but I couldn't make out what they were saying. My head hurt, and I felt cramps in my stomach. Damn alcohol. I shouldn't have drunk too much without eating enough dinner beforehand. I lifted my hand to cover my forehead, and I felt heat rising to my head. I needed some water, but first, I had to find out where I was.

Last thing I remembered was being at Sage's party in her kitchen with her and the guys. I hoped the party wasn't over yet because I normally never missed a birthday. But from the sound of it, there weren't many guests left.

I finally opened my eyes, looking straight up at the ceiling. It was dark in the room, but I knew I was in Sage's room, recognizing the five lightbulbs hanging from a wooden log attached to the ceiling.

For a moment, I laid there and tried to regain my strength and will to get off the bed, and luckily, I somehow managed to do just that. Steadying myself on the nightstand, I took a deep breath and walked toward the bedroom door to get to the voices coming from the living room.

After opening it and stepping out into the hall, the talking immediately stopped, and I looked over to the couch, seeing Sage, Jagger, and Dallas all sitting there, with no one else around.

"She's alive!" Dallas chimed, and I frowned, wondering how long I'd been out.

"What time is it?" I asked, walking toward them slowly. Jagger got up to meet me halfway and put one arm around my back to support me. "It's almost three in the morning. You missed the whole party," he told me.

"Oh, God...I'm so sorry, Sage. I should've stopped after one drink," I sighed, looking at my cousin apologetically.

She waved her hand and shrugged. Her legs were pulled up on the couch, with a blanket covering them. "You didn't miss much. Besides, these two have kept me great company. Your lover is quite good at beer pong."

I turned to look at Jagger, biting my bottom lip. "Did you have fun?" I asked in a whisper, hoping he wasn't mad for me passing out.

"Loads," he confessed, then helped me get to the couch safely. Dallas and Sage scooted over, so we would have enough space to sit as well.

"How are you feeling?" Jagger asked, and his hand came up behind me to grab a fistful of hair, massaging the back of my head.

"Better, I think. And I really didn't miss anything? Why are you guys still up?" I leaned into Jagger's hand, silently thanking him for making my head stop throbbing.

"Cleaned the apartment and then decided to watch a movie. But I'm tired. I should head back upstairs," Dallas announced.

I looked at him and nodded, then turned to Sage

to apologize once more. "I'll never drink again, I promise."

Sage laughed, then shook her head. "It's all good. I think I should head to bed too. You think you can get her back to your apartment safely?" she asked Jagger, and he nodded. "Yeah," he said, then got up from the couch. "Come on, beautiful. You need a few more hours of sleep." I hugged Sage before I got up from the couch, then looked at Dallas who took one last sip of his beer. "Goodnight."

"Night," the other three said in unison.

As we entered Jagger's apartment a few minutes later, I turned to him and leaned into his chest to hug him. He chuckled, stroking my back softly with his hands. "You need something to drink. Come on, I'll make you a tea," he offered, and I nodded without stepping away from him.

"Thank you," I murmured into his sweatshirt, and he grabbed my hand to pull me toward the kitchen.

"Always."

I sat down at the kitchen table, running my hands through my hair and sighing deeply, wondering why he kept up with me when I was trying to get sober. "You don't remember much before you blacked out, huh?" he said, amused, taking a cup out of the cupboard, and pouring water into the kettle.

"Not really. I remember us standing in the kitchen...and Sage breaking up with Joey," I recalled, but that was pretty much it.

"So, you don't remember saying something to me that might've sparked too much...joy and excitement for you to handle?"

I had no idea what he was talking about. "What do you mean?" I scowled, watching him closely.

Jagger shrugged, amusement still lingering in his eyes. "Maybe you remember the part where I asked you if you were okay…love?" He was teasing now, but nothing came to mind when he repeated those last few words.

Love. Holy fuck.

"Oh, my God…" I buried my face into my hands and felt my cheeks burn immediately. I heard him chuckle, and as I looked back up at him, he was leaning against the counter with his arms crossed over his chest.

I eyed him for a while, both of us not saying a word but trying to figure out what to say next. I told him that I loved him last night, and I was drunk. So, that would be a great excuse if it was a lie. I kept my eyes on him, studying his face, and he was doing the same. He looked way more relaxed than I was, though. Good for him. I took a deep breath, then looked down at my hands.

"I guess I've fallen in love with you," I whispered.

CHAPTER THIRTY-FOUR

Jagger

"You seem sad about it." I kept looking at her, trying to figure out what she was really thinking. Gray lifted her head, then shook it and smiled with unshed tears in her eyes. "Because it's too early, isn't it?" she asked.

My brow lifted, and I cocked my head in question. "You think so? Isn't that the one thing no one can control about love?" I walked over to her, squatting down in front of her and taking both her hands into mine. I smiled, hoping to make her feel better.

"You're amused about it, Jagger. And I was drunk. I shouldn't have said it." Her voice was shaky, almost scared. And her facial expression seemed worried as if she were about to get her heart ripped out of her chest.

"I think it was sweet. I wasn't sure you were serious at first...but drunken words are sober thoughts." I grinned. "Harlow always says that," I pointed out.

She kept her eyes on mine, and I knew she was waiting on something. Some sort of answer to her confession. I squeezed her hands, pulling both to my lips to kiss them. "We're on the same page, Gray."

Her eyes lit up, but there was still uncertainty in them. "You don't have to say that just to make me feel better. I can take it back. We should spend some more time together before we open up about our feelings." She got up from the chair, making me stand up again.

"I take it back. I have not yet fallen for you, Jagger Curtis," she mumbled, but clear enough for me to hear. I couldn't help but chuckle. Raising both eyebrows, I watched her rub her eyes and run her hands through her hair. *Well, this is amusing.*

"Not so sure you can take back things like that," I smirked.

"'Course I can. I just did." She shrugged, her eyes back in mine, wide and expressive. "I don't have feelings for you yet," she told me boldly, and I was close to laughing out loud.

"That's too bad. I was hoping to officially call you my girlfriend from now on, but that's not happening then, hm?" I teased.

"No, it's not." She crossed her arms over her chest and looked away, chewing on her bottom lip.

I waited a minute, then moved toward her. She didn't move one bit until I was close enough to put my hands on her hips and pull her even closer. "Are you done denying that you're in love with me? Because if not, I'd be more than happy to change

205

your mind while I fuck you right here on the kitchen counter," I whispered. I leaned down to kiss her neck, then the soft spot underneath her ear. "You think that would work?" I whispered against her skin and I felt her shiver.

"I...don't know," she panted, and I pressed another kiss to her neck. This time, my tongue licked her warm skin, and a moan escaped her.

That was a good enough answer for me. I picked her up by the waist and lifted her onto the counter next to us. Pulling her legs apart, I made myself comfortable between them and pressed her upper body against mine, with one hand on her lower back, and the other on the back of her head. Our lips touched, and her hands found their way to my hair, gripping it tightly and pulling me closer to her.

"I lied," she breathed against my lips.

I chuckled, breaking the kiss, and looking at her. "No shit." I grinned, pulling her shirt out of the waistband of her skirt, and taking it off so I had easier access to her bra.

My eyes moved from her breasts to her face. I had to let her know that I was in this with her. Deeply. Cupping both her cheeks in my hands, I held her head in place and looked into her eyes. "I love you, Gray. And there's no fucking way we're moving too fast. Even if, I wouldn't care. All I want is you. Now, and hopefully forever." She was the only one I had ever said those words to. The only one who deserved to hear them from me, and the only one I wanted to say the same words back to me.

Her eyes were full of lust, and there was a hint of

happiness in them. She touched one hand to mine on her cheek, then turned her face to kiss the palm of my hand softly, her eyes still on mine. "I love you too," she whispered with a soft smile. "We can make this work, right?"

"Fuck, yeah. Last thing I want is to get beat up by your brother. Didn't have a real fight in a while. Don't wanna risk it." I laughed.

My lips where back on hers and my hands tugged on her bra's clasps to unhook them. It didn't take long before her bra landed on the floor next to my feet, and my hands cupped her breasts. "You're beautiful," I told her as my lips left hers again, and with one quick look into her eyes, I lowered my head to suck on her left nipple, then the right one. Her hands were in my hair again, and by tugging on it, she made my cock throb in my pants.

"Feels so good," she moaned, and I squeezed her breasts while my tongue was circling those little nubs.

"Come here," I drawled, helping her off the counter and turning her around so she would lean over, with her ass up against my cock. She looked back at me, her bottom wiggling against me impatiently.

I moved my hand between her thighs, lifting her skirt up to her hips so I was able to pull down her panties. But before I did that, I let my fingers move over the soft, slightly wet fabric, making Gray squeeze her legs together to stop me from teasing her.

"Jagger…" she moaned, lifting her ass up into the air even higher. I smirked, pushing her legs apart and holding them open with my foot against one of hers. "I'm getting there, love. Take it easy," I told her, but she was not up for that.

"Just fuck me already," she urged.

With a quick pull on her slip, I let them fall down her legs and with my pants quickly unbuttoned, I pulled my briefs off and kicked them away. I grabbed my already hard cock and moved the tip of it between her folds.

"I'm on birth control," she said. Her eyes were on me, and I glanced at her before pushing inside her tight pussy. "Oh, God," she whimpered, and I stopped moving for a second.

"Jagger's just fine, beautiful."

She tried to laugh, but a sigh escaped. "Just fuck me already," she ordered, and I wouldn't let her ask a third time. With my hands tightly grabbing her ass, I started to pump into her as fast and hard as I could. She moved back, meeting my thrusts, and it made me feel so fucking good as well. It was after three in the morning already, but I wasn't stopping until she begged me to.

CHAPTER THIRTY-FIVE

Gray

On Monday, I was back at work and trying to paint without the thought of Jagger distracting me every two minutes. The last weekend we spent together was incredibly nice. We stayed at his place, ate a lot, watched movies, and had sex in every corner of the apartment. When I woke up this morning and got out of bed, the soreness from the day before only got worse. I wasn't mad about it, but it reminded me of the many orgasms both Jagger and I had in just two nights. He knew exactly what he had to do and where to touch me to make me come, and I learned a lot about his body too.

But before I could get a chance to imagine his cock all hard and veiny, the door to my gallery opened and every single muscle in my body tensed. Annie walked in, and just like the first time she was here, my mood somehow changed. She was dressed in all black, and the frown between her brows told me that she wasn't having a good day.

"Have you started my painting yet?" she asked without greeting me.

"Uh...no, I have not. It's next on my list, though," I told her with a smile, hoping she would lighten up too.

"I didn't express my thoughts well the first time. I see my expectations are challenging for you, so I came to tell you a little story about my family. Maybe then you'll understand what I would like you to put on that canvas," she said in a raspy voice. She sure had one or two cigarettes too many in her past, but I wasn't going to judge her because of that. It surprised me that she came to talk. She didn't seem like a woman of many words, and she didn't seem very social, either.

"That sounds great. Please, take a seat," I offered, pointing to the chairs in the corner of the room. She sat down and pulled a small notebook out of her jacket. I put down the palette and brush I was holding and sat down on the other chair. "I love hearing stories connected to the paintings I'm about to create. It really helps, and I can put the emotion into it much better," I explained.

She nodded once, then looked up from the book. "I figured. I guess I was never ready to talk about it, but you seem to be the right person for it." I didn't think so, because I wasn't a therapist, but if it meant a happy customer, I was willing to become one for an hour.

"I have two children. Well, they're grown up, but I haven't seen them since they were little kids. I never cared much about the little one, but my son, he was the only one I tried to take care of. It was hard with the husband I had at the time. Addicted and violent. It's a miracle my kids survived being around him for so long. But you must understand that my husband wasn't a bad man. He had issues. He was mentally ill but didn't want any help. I loved him so much, but I had to escape him, and all the harm he caused."

I was listening closely, and at first, I wanted to stop her from talking anymore. The story already started like a nightmare, and now I understood her vision for the painting.

"I left them both with him, all alone. There was no one who could've helped them when he was mad. No one to protect them from his vile intentions and hurtful actions. They were little kids, but I guess my oldest realized the pain his father caused his own daughter, so he packed up one day and ran away with her. I knew where they went. Where they hid from my husband. I never showed my face to them for my own safety." She stopped for a second, then let out a hard laugh. "You see, my son...he decided to become just as violent as his father."

"I'm sorry, Annie...I think I understand now," I said, hoping to not hear more of that story. I thought she would only talk about some superficial things. Maybe a simple fight between her and her husband, or a family feud. But this was more than I wanted to hear, and I needed her to stop right there.

"Him becoming violent is not even the best part." She smirked. Not sure why it was so amusing to her, but I couldn't just kick her out. I took in a deep breath and braced myself what she told me next.

"I made sure my husband knew where they lived, so he could go ask for some help. Some money and support. I couldn't give it to him, with my new man and newborn around. I watched it all from afar. That's all I was able to do. But then, one evening, and just as I thought there was a reunion between the three of them, my son..." She stopped again, and her eyes looked almost crazed.

"My son shot him. No mercy, nothing. Just pure emptiness in his eyes while he watched his own father fall to the ground with a damn bullet in his chest. Who knows how many people he has killed before with the same lack of emotions."

I couldn't move. Her story didn't seem right, and I couldn't believe it was the truth. How could a son kill his own father while his sister was watching? I should hate the guy, but something inside me told me that he wasn't the only bad guy in the story. Something must've driven him to do such a cruel thing.

"Look at him," Annie said, pulling a photograph from between the pages of her book. "I hope it helps with the painting," she added, putting down the picture of her son onto the small table between us. With no other words, Annie got up and left my gallery. As I heard the door close, I felt release come over me, but there was still uncertainty and an unwell feeling inside of me.

I reached for the photograph, holding it up closer to see the face of the little boy on it. It was black and white, his face showed little to no emotion, even though the corners of his mouth were turned upward slightly. His eyes said a lot compared to the

212

rest of him. There were panic, pain, and helplessness in them, and his hair stuck up on all sides, not being brushed in a while.

Then, something on the boy's face caught my attention. A scar, from under his ear down to the middle of the side of his neck suddenly became the focus of the picture. I couldn't look away, because it reminded me so much of something I'd seen a lot in the past months. That scar was part of the man I loved, and my heart clenched at the thought of Jagger being the main character of the story Annie told me minutes ago.

CHAPTER THIRTY-SIX

Jagger

It surprised me how intelligent, yet incredibly detestable a person could be. My mother was no exception, and with her standing in front of my car as I turned the corner, I knew she wasn't here to show her nice side after years of being gone. I even thought about turning around and leaving, but if I did that, she might never leave again.

Walking toward her, I decided not to create drama. "How did you find me?" I asked calmly, shoving both my hands into my front pockets. She eyed me for a while, then tilted her head and shrugged.

"Internet," she simply said. "Aren't you glad to see me?"

"Fuck, no," I spit, then quickly tried to relax again. No fucking drama needed with this woman around. Honestly, it was no surprise to see her here. I'm just glad she's not in Hastings, hunting Harlow down. Ann never cared for Harlow. Just packed her stuff and left after coming back from the hospital, leaving her alone with me and fucking Dean.

"What are you doing here?" Not that I cared, I just wanted her to move along.

"Can't a mother visit her son after not hearing from him in years? Oh, Jagger, I thought I raised you well enough."

"Apparently not." I sighed. "I have work to attend to," I pointed out, but she wasn't taking the hint.

"Turns out I don't live far from here. But before I came here, I tried to find your father back in Nevada. I figured he'd still be there after you took your sister to Nebraska. I quickly found out he was dead," she said in an amused tone. "Shot by his own damn son," she added.

"Who told you?" I asked, cursing myself for letting her this close now.

"Didn't have to ask anyone."

"Jesus Christ," I ran my hands through my hair, gritting my teeth and trying to stay calm. "You need to leave," I told her, now looking at her again.

She laughed at me and shook her head. "I can't. There's this wonderful artist down by the railways creating an intense artwork for our family story. I think you know her…ginger hair, sweet face…"

Gray.

"What did you tell her?" I warned, grabbing the keys out of my pocket, and stalking over to the car door. "I swear to God…if she's upset because of you, then—"

"Then, what? Will you kill me too? Just like you did with your own father?" She seemed to enjoy

215

this, and she was lucky no one was around to hear her say those things. The last thing I needed was for the whole town to know that I pulled a fucking gun on my father.

"We're not done here," I promised her, then drove off to hopefully find Gray at her workplace.

***

"Gray," I called out as I entered her gallery, and I quickly found her sitting in one of the chairs she had in a corner. She was holding something in her hand, but the way she was sitting, I couldn't quite make out what it was. I quickly walked over, squatting down in front of her and looking up into her face. She looked worried and confused, with her eyes full of questions.

"Hey," I said softly, lowering my eyes to the picture now. It was me she was holding on to, and the hate I felt toward my mother grew with each second that passed.

"Is it true?" Her voice was quiet, almost not audible for me. I wasn't going to lie, but I wasn't asking her what Ann told her, either.

"I didn't know she was in town. Hell, I haven't heard from her in over twenty years. Whatever she said…just know that I'm not who she said I was." My attempt to make her feel better didn't work, and she kept looking at the picture in her hands.

"Gray, love…" I whispered, squeezing her thighs lightly. "Let me explain, okay?"

Slowly, her eyes met mine and the tears started to fall. "I should be afraid of you. I should hate

216

you," she sobbed, and that was one reason why I wanted to chase Ann away from Newton.

"I know. And you have every right to. But I promise you, Gray…that's not who I am. I can explain. I made mistakes. Lots of them. But one thing I know for sure is that I don't ever want to push you away from me. I love you," I told her, and another sob escaped her chest.

She didn't speak, and that was the best opportunity for me to take her into my embrace and comfort her, even if she wasn't sure what to think about what Ann told her. I wanted her close, and I wanted her to keep trusting me. I pulled her to me, as close as possible, and I wrapped my arms around her as tight as ever. She hid her face into my neck, and I caressed the back of her head with one hand.

"Let me explain," I repeated, and she slowly shook her head. Pulling back from me, I hoped I didn't feel the shake of her head for real.

"I need to be alone for a while. You have work in ten minutes," she reminded me, but I didn't feel like leaving.

"You're upset. I won't leave you here without being sure that you're okay," I told her, but she shook her head. "Please leave, Jagger."

At this point, I couldn't read her face like before. Her emotions left, and I had no chance of knowing what she was thinking. "You're upset," I repeated, but she didn't want to hear that.

"I'm upset because of you, Jagger! Leave!" Her voice was shaky, and her bottom lip seemed to tremble. "Don't make this worse," she whispered.

I had to if I wanted even one small chance to

make it all better again. If I kept pushing her to talk to me, I might as well give myself the move-on-card. The least I could do was to give her space. Some time to think.

Standing back up I sighed and reached out my hand to brush the tears off her cheek. Then, bending down, I kissed her forehead softly. "I love you, Gray. I'll be waiting," I whispered, then left her gallery, not knowing when I would see her again.

EPILOGUE

Jagger

I knew she received the note I left her before driving back to Hastings at the end of March. It's been exactly one hundred seventy days since I've seen Gray, and I hoped with each day that passed that a call or text from her would come in. I didn't know what she told her brother and cousin, but from their texts from some weeks ago, it looked like they thought Gray and I were in a long-distance relationship. I wasn't sure what we were, but I knew that I still loved her. With all my heart.

I left Newton because of Harlow giving me the great news about Ann showing up in Hastings and causing a little bit of trouble. I knew Ann wasn't there to mess around with Low, but I wasn't happy with them being around each other, especially Hunter being present too.

Since I was back in Hastings, I spent my nights in Hunter's old trailer, and by day, I helped them out at the diner. Their baby was growing, and

Harlow started to feel weaker each day. That was one fair reason to leave Newton. But the real reason was to give Gray some space. What Ann told her was rough, and I wanted to give her the time to reflect on it while I wasn't around. If I had stayed, there weren't many places she could hide from me besides her gallery and her apartment. Before I left, I kept working for Dallas, and Gray never visited him or Sage at their apartments. I was blocking her way, and that wasn't my intention.

So, leaving was the only good option. Ann somehow managed to stick around longer than I wanted her to. She showed up a few times a month, hoping to speak to me and Harlow at once, but I always sent her packing. Harlow didn't need that stress right now, and I wanted the baby to be healthy once it's born.

"You miss her, right?" Harlow's voice was comforting, but I wasn't sure I felt like talking about Gray. I was sitting at an empty booth after the diner closed, drinking a beer, and contemplating the past months. Harlow sat down next to me, squeezing in her belly. I looked down at it, then put my hand over her belly, caressing it softly.

"I can't wait to meet him," I said quietly, smiling at the feel of a small kick. Harlow smiled brightly. "He's excited to meet you too. He only ever kicks when he hears your voice. It's weird." She laughed, and I couldn't help a grin. "His father is probably already scaring the shit outta this little guy," I joked, kissing my sister's temple.

Harlow's smile softened, and she grabbed my hand off her belly. "You ignored my question, Jag. I know you don't like talking about it, but it helps. Gray's unsure. What Ann did was horrible. It wasn't for her to tell her. But I'm sure Gray isn't mad at you. She seemed like an understanding person, and I bet once she's heard your side of the story, she'll be able to trust you again."

Sighing, I looked at my sister's hopeful face. Low was good at forgiving people who have done her wrong, and she quickly knew when someone had that trait too. I knew Gray wasn't angry. She got pulled away from me by someone that had no right in doing so.

"She hasn't texted or called. I sometimes wake up with the urge to drive back to her and make everything better, but I don't want to push her if she's not ready to see me again."

Harlow's brow arched, and I knew she didn't approve of my words. "If anything, I think she's just waiting for you to go back to her. Jagger…you love her. It's not fair to her and it's not fair to you to keep this distance," Harlow said.

I thought about her words, wondering if that was all it took for me to get into my car and run after the girl I fell in love with so deeply just before disaster struck. Eyeing Harlow, I started to nod, then ran a hand through my hair. "You're right," I admitted.

"I'm always right." And with Harlow's wise words, I started to plan out my return to Newton, and how to get the girl back I couldn't stop thinking about.

To be continued…

Jagger & Gray's Playlist

Perfect Strangers – Jonas Blue
Don't Look Back in Anger – Oasis
For What It's Worth – Liam Gallagher
Something Just Like This – The Chainsmokers,
Coldplay
Young Folks – Peter Bjorn and John
Runaways – The Killers
Talk – Coldplay
Home – Machine Gun Kelly
Say (All I Need) – OneRepublic
Satellite – Nickelback
Love Remains The Same – Gavin Rossdale
New Religion – The Heydaze
Tongue Tied – Grouplove
Heavy – Linkin Park, Kiiara

Acknowledgements

I realized speaking my mind, if I don't do it through a character I created, isn't easy for me. So, writing this is going to be harder than writing a whole book. In fact, this is harder than writing one single chapter for me, so I'll keep it short and simple.

I want to thank everyone involved with this book. From friend to editor, to reader.

A very special thanks to Enny, Domino, Cayla, Nikki, and Marissa.

About The Author

Vanessa Siena is a twenty-something-year-old student with Italian roots living in Switzerland, where she was born and raised. Spending most of her free time as a teenager writing, she one day decided to upload her first official work "HUNTER" on Wattpad, where she reached over 100'000 reads in less than five months. When she's not writing, she plays bass guitar, reads novels and likes to eat to pass the time. Being very inspired by the '80s, rock bands from that time are always playing in the background.

Social Media Links

Instagram:
https://www.instagram.com/authorvanessasiena/

Wattpad:
https://www.wattpad.com/user/harlovv

Join our Reader Group on Facebook and don't miss out on meeting our authors and entering epic giveaways!

Limitless Reading

Where reading a book
is your first step to becoming
limitless...

LIMITLESS PUBLISHING *Reader Group*

Join today! *"Where reading a book is your first step to becoming limitless..."*